AN INCONVENIENT CHRISTMAS

Sara R. Turnquist

To Tina –
Happy Reading!
Sara R. T.
Psalm 139:23-24

An Inconvenient Christmas
by Sara Turnquist

This is a work of fiction. Names, places, characters, and events are fictitious in every regard. Any similarities to actual events and persons, living or dead, are purely coincidental. Any trademarks, service marks, product names, or named features are assumed to be the property of their respective owners, and are used only for reference. There is no implied endorsement if any of these terms are used. Except for review purposes, the reproduction of this book in whole or part, electronically or mechanically, constitutes a copyright violation.

For my children, in whose eyes I enjoy the Christmas season as if for the first time.

CHAPTER ONE

It's In The Air

AMANDA MILLER TIED another red ribbon into a bow on the fireplace mantle. Hopefully she was nearing the end. As much as she loved decorating, it could become tedious.

Hands slid around her waist, and she was pulled against a strong chest. Her husband's masculine scent filled her nostrils, and she leaned into him. How had she become so blessed?

He planted a kiss to the side of her face. "Any chance we can slip away?"

She turned her head to peer at him. Was he serious?

A playful gleam in his eye answered her

unspoken question.

Her lips tugged upward. How she loved this man! Laying hands atop his on her stomach, she relished the feel of him. His strong arms and secure hands were well known to her. Worked by ranch life, they were capable and calloused. Yet gentle as well.

"Momma," a little voice called from across the room.

Pulled from her reverie, Amanda's attention fixed on the small girl toddling toward them.

Reluctantly, she pulled free of Brandon's embrace and, squatting, put arms out to receive the girl. "That's it, come to Momma."

"Momma."

It didn't matter that Louise said the word a million times a day; it was glorious.

A grin broke out across the child's face, creating dimples in her chubby cheeks.

The wriggling bundle, teetering with every step, somehow made it to Amanda's outstretched hands before falling.

She lifted her daughter, swinging her into the air and kissing the baby-fine skin. When she stopped, she caught Brandon's eye.

"I see you've forgiven her for saying 'Daddy' first." He reached forth a hand for Louise to capture it.

She did, pulling at his fingers.

"I don't know what you're talking about." Amanda spoke to Brandon, but she looked at Louise and spoke in a sing-song voice. "Do we, Louise Ann?

We don't know what Daddy is saying."

"Oh, Louise knows good and well."

The child grinned and pulled two of Brandon's fingers into her mouth.

He jerked them back with a catch in his breath.

"Oh, no!" Amanda became instantly concerned. "Did she bite you?"

Brandon looked at his hand and nodded. "It's not so bad."

"I'm sorry. I think she has teeth coming in. She's been biting everything."

His brows furrowed, and he let out a concerned grunt.

"Yesterday, Samuel brought Daisy closer so Louise could pet her. And what we thought was going to be a kiss from Louise turned out to be an attempt to bite the poor dog's ear."

A chuckle escaped Brandon. Was it something to laugh about?

"It wasn't funny." She widened her eyes. "The dog could have been hurt."

He cleared his throat and tightened his mouth. "No, of course."

Amanda shifted Louise to her other hip. "I don't want her to become a biter."

Brandon furrowed his brows and let out a long breath.

Amanda fingered the curls in the child's soft hair.

"Let's not jump to that while she is still teething.

But we *can* watch out and make sure she doesn't hurt anyone."

Was that truly all they could do? What more would she suggest? Perhaps Brandon was right.

"After all, she comes by that feistiness pretty honest. It's one of her mother's more…intriguing qualities." His voice was husky as he put an arm around her, drawing her near.

Amanda's head cleared of all but him. She was helpless when he spoke to her like this.

He pressed a kiss to her forehead, his breath lingering on her skin.

The door opened, and Louise wriggled for freedom, but Amanda didn't let her escape.

"Aw, Ma, do ya have to?"

Amanda spun toward Samuel. Where had he been? Shouldn't he have been helping her with the decorations? She opened her mouth.

"Did you finish with the horses?" Brandon's chest vibrated as he spoke.

The horses? What did Brandon have Samuel doing with the horses?

"Sure did." Samuel grinned.

Amanda clamped her mouth shut. She would not disrespect Brandon in front of her son, but this was not over.

"Good. I think Cutie and Slim are going fishing."

Samuel's eyes lit up. His gaze shifted toward Amanda.

"Go on." She pulled away from Brandon and set Louise on the floor with her blocks. "You don't want to miss them."

A clapping of the door on its hinges was his only response.

Standing, she eyed Brandon, brow raised.

He tilted his head. "What?"

"You have him working with the horses?"

"It's good for him."

"That's what you said about mucking stalls."

"Was I wrong?"

Amanda crossed her arms. Dare she concede? Could she not? Why did she want to keep her boy close to her skirts? Why must Brandon constantly be pushing him further away?

Reaching out, he pulled her toward his chest. "You know I'm right."

She looked away and bit at her lip. "Maybe."

He hooked her chin with a finger. "Probably."

Her lips twinged at the edges. She fought the smile. "Don't push it."

His mouth curved upward, but his brown eyes rested on her lips. "I might just take the risk." Leaning forward, he pressed his lips to hers.

Would she ever become numb to this feeling? This excitement, this heat coursing through her? Or would his kisses thrill her for as long as they both should live?

She hoped so.

His arms wrapped around her back, and he tilted

his head to deepen the contact.

But after a few moments of bliss, she pulled back.

Brandon traced a finger down the side of her face. "Is it time for Louise's nap?"

If only…

No, she couldn't get distracted.

"I'm afraid not. And I need to talk to you." She drew farther back.

"Oh?" He watched her every movement.

She glanced at Louise. Had she caught hold of something dangerous? There was no end to the child's mischief.

The small girl sat where Amanda had set her. For once.

Amanda reached for the box of ornaments, picking it up and, moving toward the dining space, placing it on the table.

"Everything all right?" Brandon called from where he had remained.

She pushed her hair back and sighed. How to broach the subject? Why was she so nervous? Couldn't she tell Brandon anything?

She turned toward him and leaned against the table.

"I know that look." His brows furrowed.

What look? How did she look? Did her features display her worry? Her trepidation? It would be best to just be out with it.

Drawing in a deep breath, she closed her eyes

briefly and then met his gaze. "Cook and Uncle Owen won't be coming for Christmas."

"Oh." He set his hands on his hips. "That's not at all what I expected. But it is their first Christmas as man and wife."

Amanda nodded.

"But that can't be what has you so worried." He crossed the room, closing the distance between them.

She chewed on her lip.

"What is it?" His eyes were caring. Concerned.

Guilt filled her. She had to tell him.

"Are you nervous about making the big meal alone?"

Her eyes widened. That had not occurred to her.

"Oh, no." He gently clasped her arms. "Forget I said that. I'll help. Anyway I can."

She waved a hand between them. It wouldn't be easy, but she would manage. "It's not that."

"Then what is it?" He rubbed his larger hands along her upper arms.

"A letter came."

"A letter?"

She reached into the pocket of her apron and pulled out the lightly crinkled envelope. "From your parents."

Brandon's jaw clamped shut. She watched as the muscles twitched.

How long had it been since he had heard from his parents? Years? Decades? And all of a sudden a letter comes? Why now?

"When?"

"About two hours ago. While you were…"

He nodded. "Out with the cattle."

She searched his face, holding the envelope between them, ready for him to take it.

But he just stared at it.

"Did you read it?" His eyes met hers, and there was a darkness to their depths she had not seen in a long time.

"No." She pushed the word out.

His hands on her arms had grown limp.

Should she insist he take the letter? Or offer to read it for him? Was this something *he* needed to do?

Louise let out a cry.

Amanda looked in her direction. There was a block in her hand that was well wet.

Louise broke out in fierce tears.

Had she been chewing on the block and hurt her gums? Or bitten her finger by accident?

Amanda glanced at Brandon, pushing the letter toward him. She could no longer give him time to think.

Brandon stood, holding out his hand with the envelope.

She rushed to Louise and picked her up. The child immediately snuggled into Amanda's chest, her cries now muffled by Amanda's shoulder.

Amanda rubbed her back. "It's all right, sweet girl."

As the crying let up, she shifted the child to her hip and examined her fingers.

"What happened? Did you bite your finger?"

Sure enough, there was a reddened place on the forefinger of her right hand.

"Oh, my baby!" Amanda put a light kiss on the tiny finger. "There. All better."

Louise looked at her finger and then at Amanda. Her cries waned as if she wasn't sure what to do. But they soon vanished as the small girl stuck her finger toward Amanda's mouth again.

"Momma kiss."

Amanda grabbed her little hand and pressed several kisses to the finger. "Yes, Momma kiss it. Make it all better."

Louise giggled.

Then Louise stuck her hand in the direction of the dining room. "Daddy kiss!"

Amanda spun toward Brandon.

He stood just as she had left him, staring at the unopened letter.

She moved toward him. Drawing close, she put a hand on his shoulder. "Do you need some time alone?"

Shaking his head, he met her gaze. "No, I need you."

What could she do? What could she offer him? She stopped herself. That was the old Amanda. He needed her support. Her love.

"And I am right here with you."

He nodded.

She reached for a dining chair and pulled it out.

Brandon all but fell into it.

Grabbing for the chair next to him, she sat with Louise on her lap.

His eyes met hers, and she nodded.

He slid a finger under the flap and tore through the seal.

Freeing a hand, she squeezed his arm in reassurance.

Pulling the papers free, he unfolded them. His eyes drifted over the writing.

He let out a long breath.

"It's not possible."

Brandon pulled back on the reins, causing Candy to slow.

He watched the cattle shift into the northern pasture. But his thoughts were not on the animals. Not truly.

They were on that letter.

His parents had never written him. He had not heard a word from them since he left Richmond. And he had never looked back. Well, not often.

Now. They chose now.

Why?

His life was good. Truly good.

He had a thriving ranch, a wonderful family, and an amazing marriage that he never would have anticipated being so good.

Now this.

And it was only the beginning.

For they would be here in a week.

It had been many years since Brandon had reconciled himself to the fact that he quite possibly would never see his mother and father again. He had mourned that loss.

Having to revisit it was…uncomfortable at the very least.

But there was nothing for it. They were coming, and he could do nothing to prevent it.

Had they arranged it this way?

He wagered so.

Their letter arrived one day too late to send a telegram to stop them from starting their journey.

Would he have stopped them?

He didn't know.

Perhaps he should be thankful he didn't have that decision to make.

Yet he wasn't.

"Boss?" a loud voice called to him.

Brandon jerked his head in the direction of the sound.

Cutie rode toward him.

"Yeah?"

The ranch hand slowed his own horse as he approached. "Did you want us to move the second herd to the back pasture?"

"Sure."

Cutie shifted. Almost as if he were uncertain

about his next move.

Brandon didn't have time for this. "You need something?"

The ranch hand frowned.

Perhaps he was harsher than he'd intended.

"Sorry, Cutie. I'm just…my thoughts are elsewhere today."

Cutie nodded.

"Was there something you wanted to ask?"

"It's just that…well, me and the boys were kind of hoping that…the thing is…"

"Saints alive, spit it out!"

Cutie's face colored, and Brandon regretted snapping again.

"There's a Christmas dance in town next week. And we were hoping you might see fit to let us go."

A dance? Was that all? Brandon let out a laugh. "That's it? You fellas all want the evening off?"

Cutie shrugged, his color deepening. "Yeah."

Brandon slapped his thigh. "Go ahead. Just don't have too much fun." He gave his ranch hand a wink.

"'Course not." One side of Cutie's mouth quirked upward. With that, he turned his mount, steering the painted mare toward the far pasture.

A Christmas dance. Brandon gazed toward the house.

Amanda was in the yard chasing Louise. They both laughed. Not only could he see it, Louise's shrieks were audible, even at this distance.

Should he take Amanda to that dance? It had been a while since he'd made such an overture.

Perhaps Cook and Uncle Owen could mind Louise and Samuel.

But then, his parents would be here.

How might that change things?

Oh, but how...

The sounds of Louise's giggles entranced Amanda. She would never tire of that music. And to know that it was her big brother who brought out such delight...such joy to a momma's heart.

Even though her children were in another room, separated by a wall, nothing could disguise their playful engagement.

"Children truly are a gift from the Lord."

Amanda faced the older woman kneading dough. "Yes. They are."

"When will we hear more little feet around here?"

Her face warmed. She reached toward her bowl of beans for the next one. Gripping it firmly, she snapped it.

Cook's stifled laughter shook her frame.

Amanda threw a bean at her.

"You best not make a mess in my kitchen." Cook's face became stern.

Had she upset the woman? She looked more

closely into the features she had come to know so well.

There was a glint in Cook's eye that was impossible to miss.

Amanda grinned.

Cook winked and focused on her work, and began humming.

There were so many things Amanda had come to enjoy about her life. These times with Cook, whether they were confiding in each other, in lively conversation, or companionable silence at work, were definitely one of them.

A few minutes passed as they continued on task, preparing food for the evening meal.

Amanda snuck a peek at Cook. What did she know of Brandon's past? Of his parents? Dare Amanda ask? How to broach the subject?

Cook smiled and looked at Amanda. "I think Louise is going to nap well today."

"Hope so." A yawn escaped.

Cook quirked an eyebrow. "Something keeping you up at night?"

Amanda furrowed her brows. "Not what you think."

"Oh?"

Tossing another bean in the pot, Amanda leaned forward and thrust out her response. "No."

"Is Louise getting up at night again?" Cooks features rearranged into something akin to sympathy.

Amanda shook her head.

"Well, don't keep me guessing, child!"

Looking at her for a moment, Amanda gauged the older woman's reaction.

Cook paused and set her full attention on Amanda.

"Has Brandon not told you?" She narrowed her eyes.

"Told me what?"

Amanda quirked a brow. Brandon told Uncle Owen and Cook everything. How had they not heard about the letter?

"I don't like that look," the older woman warned, rising. "You best tell me now, or I'll march out to that field and drag that husband of yours in here."

Amanda stuck an arm out. Was Cook not speaking in jest? Did she truly not know? "I'll tell you."

Cook sat, mumbling. Something about yanking teeth. She crossed her arms and leveled her gaze on Amanda. Would she not return to her work?

Amanda swallowed. She certainly did not intend to put so much pressure on the moment. Sucking in a breath, she pressed on. "Brandon received a letter."

Cook's expression did not change.

"From his parents."

Still no visible reaction.

"And they are coming for Christmas. They'll be here in four days."

"Is that all?" Cook uncrossed her arms and set her hands back to forming the bread.

"All? You speak as though they correspond regularly."

Cook's hazel eyes were on hers again. She opened her mouth and then closed it. Did she have something to add?

Amanda wiped her hands on her apron. "What? Do you know something?"

"No." Cook stood, taking the loaf pan to the oven.

Then Amanda was presented with the woman's back as she opened and closed the small door.

Curious. Very curious.

When she didn't turn again, Amanda pursed her lips. Something wasn't right here.

"What do you know?"

Cook spun, wringing her hands in a cloth. "Nothing."

"Cook…" Were they not better friends than this?

The woman scanned the kitchen, looking everywhere but at Amanda.

"All right, all right! I can't do it." She stepped back to where she and Amanda had been settled. Flopping into the chair, she pointed a finger in Amanda's face. "But you best not breathe a word of this."

Amanda nodded.

"We got a letter about a month ago."

"You…!"

Cook put her hands up. "Shhh!"

Amanda lowered her voice. "A month ago?"

"Yes."

"Do you know why now? After all this time?"

Cook shrugged, sitting back. "Mrs. Miller didn't say. Maybe it's time. People change as they age. The things that once seemed so important aren't so important anymore."

Amanda nodded. This had occurred to her, too. And she prayed it would be so. That his father was prepared to reconcile.

"Lord knows, it's about time those stubborn men put their wills to the side."

"What do you mean?" Amanda rose and set the beans on the counter.

"Brandon's father has his part in this, that's for sure. But you didn't think it was all him, did you?"

What was she saying? That there was more to Brandon's role in the falling out than he had shared? "I suppose I didn't think too much about it," she lied.

Cook shot her a look.

"All I know is what Brandon has told me."

"There are two sides to every story, you know."

"I suppose." What had Brandon left out? Dare she ask him? But she had promised Cook she wouldn't share. How else would she bring it up?

Cook slapped her knees. "I'd best get started on the ham."

Amanda nodded. "I need to check on Louise. No doubt it's time for that nap."

Sweeping past Amanda, Cook began her routine dance around the kitchen. That was Amanda's cue to get out of her way. She slipped from the room and stepped into the great room to find both Samuel and Louise asleep on the floor.

She folded her arms in front of her. If only life could always be so simple.

Brandon scuffed the bottoms of his boots against the wooden planks that made up the walkway. And he continued to wait. He stared down the main stretch into town and watched.

The town was decked out in greenery, highlighted here and there by red ribbons. They had done their part to make everything festive. Still, the spirit of the season must have missed him as it made its way further west.

He had yet to come across anything special enough to give Amanda. And he needed to find something fantastic. There was little doubt she would find the perfect gift for him. That must be her hidden talent—giving gifts.

Letting out a deep breath, he folded his arms in front of his chest and paced toward the telegraph office. There was a myriad of postings hung there.

His heart skipped a beat when he saw the wanted poster of Kid Antrim. What was he calling himself now? Billy something... Oh yes, Billy the Kid. Brandon frowned at the drawing of the man whose visage still visited his darkest dreams.

Tearing his eyes away, he scanned the other

writings. The most recent copy of the town gazette had an article about the upcoming Christmas dance, the event of the season. He had not yet spoken with Cook about minding Louise and Samuel that evening. What of his parents? Would they go to the dance? Or would they be insulted that Brandon had planned an evening away for him and Amanda?

He grumbled. There was no easy answer. His parents were fairly unknown to him now.

Moving back to the road, he glanced at the sun's position in the sky. Why had he arrived with so much time to spare? Had he been concerned the stage would come early? It never was. Perhaps, had he not come, it would have been today.

That was nonsense.

Still, he was left waiting.

Wasn't that all he had done these past five days since the letter arrived—wait?

None of the answers he sought would be forthcoming in the meantime. No, his parents, more likely, his father, was the key to all of it.

The tell-tale thundering piqued his senses. He turned his head to gaze down the strip of buildings, in the direction the coach would appear. How long would it be now? His heart beat wildly in his chest. Was he so nervous?

Moments later, the coach appeared, right on schedule, rounding the corner at the end of Main Street. The coachman pulled hard at the reins, and the horses slowed.

Brandon closed his eyes. *Lord, I don't know what to say. I don't know what to do. But here I am. May I be responsible with my words, with my actions. Give me strength.*

The coach stopped, surrounded by a cloud of dust.

Still, Brandon did not move. Could he?

Jumping down, the coachman reached for the latch. "Wharton City!" he yelled into the compartment before jerking the small door open.

A tall man with broad shoulders, a slender frame, and gray hair looked out. He was well-dressed in fine traveling clothes. Though he scanned the area, bushy brows furrowed, he soon descended the small step and reached in to assist the other passengers.

A young woman stepped out. And the next to appear was a face Brandon would never forget as long as he lived. Though age had salted her dark hair and caused her frame to sag slightly, her features were as kind as ever, her eyes as bright as he remembered—Mother.

Brandon let out a breath.

Once her feet touched the boards, she set her hand on the older man's arm. Was that?

The years had not been good to Father. His hair had grayed, but so had his features. They were set and grim. But just as Brandon remembered, he appeared generally displeased with everything around him.

They spoke to one another briefly, and Father motioned to the driver as the man pulled their things from the top of the coach.

Shouldn't Brandon help? To do that, he would need to step forward, make himself known. And his feet just wouldn't work.

Mother scanned the area, her mouth moving. What was she saying?

At last, her eyes landed on him, and she smiled. She reached for Father's arm and pulled at him, pointing in Brandon's direction.

Father's gaze leveled on Brandon. He scowled, but something passed in his eyes. Something Brandon wasn't sure he could identify.

Brandon wasn't quite certain how he got there, but he soon found himself standing in front of his parents.

"Brandon," Mother said, taking him in. "My, look at you." She opened her arms.

It was both awkward and easy to embrace her.

As he pulled back, he did not miss the unsteady half-smile on her face.

"You have changed." Father's voice was deep. His words did not sound like a compliment.

Brandon nodded. "We all have." His voice came out tight. Amanda wouldn't like that. It might very well be up to him to set the right tone.

Father's mouth became a thin line.

Silence fell between them. A tense silence.

Mother looked from Brandon to Father then back to Brandon. "Where shall we have them put our things?"

"I'll pull my cart around."

"I won't hear of it," Father said. His features were hard. "Did you not read the letter? We will stay at your town's hotel." His gaze drifted down the main stretch.

"Wharton City doesn't have a hotel."

Father's brows met. "Surely you must have something."

"There is a boarding house that serves as a sort of hotel."

"Then we shall inquire after—"

"But I insist that you stay in my home."

"Absolutely not. There cannot be enough room for—"

Heat flashed through Brandon. "Though I may not have a grand house, there is plenty of space for you both to stay there comfortably."

Father lowered his brows. Was he preparing another argument? He opened his mouth to speak.

Mother laid a hand on Father's arm and met Brandon's gaze. "We would be happy to stay at your home if you are certain we won't be a bother."

Brandon swallowed the words he wanted to speak. And instead said, "No, it won't be any trouble at all."

"But—" Father started.

Mother turned toward him.

Brandon could not see her face, as she now had her back to him. They spoke in hushed tones. He watched with wide eyes for a moment. Mother had never spoken against Father before. What was this new dynamic? Was he intruding?

He stepped to where the coachman had stacked the bags and trunks. "Which of these belong to Mr. and Mrs. Miller?"

The man quirked a brow at him. "All of it."

"All of it?" Brandon searched for the other passengers. "But what of the young lady who…and the…"

The driver shook his head.

"All of it."

A nod was his only answer.

Brandon pushed out a breath. "All right."

He looked back toward his parents.

They seemed to be having tense words. Father spoke less and less. Finally, he nodded.

Mother put a hand in the crook of Father's elbow and he led her to where Brandon stood with their things.

"We would be…honored to stay at your home," Father bit out.

Brandon attempted to disguise his surprise, but was perhaps unable to. His eyes widened, but he kept his mouth clamped shut. "Very well. I'll get my wagon."

He turned and moved off.

What kind of visit was he in for?

CHAPTER TWO

Yuletide Troubles

BRANDON REACHED INTO the back of the wagon as Father helped Mother down. The ride to the ranch had been anything but pleasant. It had been quiet, to be sure, but it was an awkward silence. What few words did pass between them were tense.

Father did not like the bumpiness of the ride — couldn't the township afford to better keep the roads? Or perhaps it was the wheels that were in ill repair?

Why did Brandon have to live so far outside of the town, small as it was? Didn't he fear for his safety? It didn't seem wise.

How could Brandon respond?

So he didn't.

And Father's words melted into a series of grunts and grumbles.

Now he was home; the arduous journey was behind them. Brandon pulled the first trunk toward himself. Heavy. He attempted to lower it gently, but the weight of it carried it much faster than he could manage.

It crashed to the ground.

As Brandon righted himself, he inspected the casing. Thankfully, nothing was damaged. Well, nothing but perhaps his pride.

Father appeared around the side of the cart. "What the devil are you doing?"

Brandon could do nothing but look at him.

"Did you try to unload that yourself?"

Glancing at the trunk, now clouded with dust, Brandon refused to meet Father's gaze. His face burned. Father was right. The driver at the station had assisted him with loading everything. Why had he neglected to take care now? Had he not realized?

But he had. Was he trying to prove something?

"Did you hear me?"

Brandon looked at his father.

The older man ran a hand down his face.

Mother stepped around him. "Do you not have workers who could assist?" Her voice was soft.

Shoving a hand through his hair, Brandon took a step back from the trunk. "Yes." He let out a breath.

Mother's hand touched his arm. Had she moved closer? "Then let's leave this to them."

He caught her eyes. They were kind. She was ever the peacemaker. Nodding, he set his hands to his hips.

"Come," Mother said as she put a hand on his elbow. "Show us your home."

His mouth twitched as he laid a hand on his mother's, but a smile was not forthcoming. He chanced a glance at Father. The man's steely gaze never left him.

It was no matter.

"Let's start with the house." Brandon forced a smile onto his face. "Amanda will be excited to meet you."

Mother nodded and picked up step with Brandon as he moved toward the homestead.

He could only guess that Father would follow.

As they approached the porch steps, the front door opened, and Amanda glided out, Louise on her hip and Samuel behind her.

She had done some work to prepare the children and herself. The top of Louise's curly blonde hair had been pulled back with two blue ribbons and she now wore her best dress—a matching blue flouncy thing trimmed in lace.

Samuel's hair had been slicked back and down. He pulled at his church clothes even then. A fine, pressed rust-colored shirt and his best brown pants. The picture he made caused Brandon's smile to become genuine. How the boy struggled with his dress clothes.

Amanda must not have had the time she would have liked on her own appearance, but as always, she was lovely. She, likewise, had donned a church dress—pink with a modest neckline. It hugged her figure in the right places until the snug waistline gave way to a full skirt. Her hair had been curled and pulled up. A rarity. It elongated her neck and gave him thoughts he might shouldn't have in front of his parents.

He guided his parents the rest of the way up the stairs and they stopped just short of where Amanda and the children stood.

"Mother, Father, I would like to introduce you to my wife, Amanda Miller, and my children, Samuel and Louise."

Mother reached toward Amanda. "It is good to meet you."

Amanda took her proffered hand. "And you. I have heard so much about you."

Brandon shot her a look, but Amanda wasn't catching it. Her gaze was on his mother.

Mother stepped closer and set her fingers gently on Louise's cheek. "My, she is adorable."

"Thank you," Amanda said, turning so as to put Louise closer to her grandmother. "I often wonder if she looks like Brandon when he was young.

"Oh, yes," Mother said. "These curls are yours. But those eyes are Brandon's for certain."

"Are *both* of these children yours, Brandon?" Father interjected.

Brandon's gaze jerked to his father's placid face.

Mother and Amanda fell silent.

What must Amanda be thinking? How must Samuel feel?

"Yes," Brandon said firmly.

Father's brow shot up. "This boy here? Why, he must be what? Six? Seven years old? Were you not just married two summers ago?" Ever the inquisitor. He held himself as if he were in a courtroom, addressing a witness. Stepping toward Samuel, Father peered down without so much as slouching.

A fire lit in Brandon's stomach. How dare Father do this.

"Charles," Mother said. "Is this necess—"

"Whose child is he? Some orphan you took in?" Father's eyes narrowed.

Brandon ground his teeth. Where were his thoughts? His words? Nothing was forthcoming.

"He is *my* son." Amanda stepped forward, grabbing Samuel's hand and pulling him away from the man who leered at him.

Father looked her up and down. "I see." Then he turned to Brandon. "How…gracious of you, son." Then he turned his back on the pair as if they no longer deserved his time.

He didn't fool Brandon. What he meant was 'how naïve.' Father had thought Amanda to have had Samuel out of wedlock and Brandon had pity on her and her child. His lips curled and his nails bit into his palms. Heat suffused his body.

"Samuel is the son of my first husband." Amanda's voice shook as she spoke. But it gained strength. "My *dead* first husband."

Father turned and his eyes met hers. "Hmm." His head tilted down as he assessed her once more, but he said nothing further. After some moments, he turned to his wife.

"Are we to tarry out on this dusty porch?" His eyes flicked to Brandon. "Or will we be invited inside this…house?"

Brandon's vision wavered. Did he not intend to apologize? Did he not regret the things he had insinuated about Brandon's wife?

He opened his mouth. What would come, he wasn't certain.

Amanda's voice filled the space that he'd intended for his retort. "Please, Mr. Miller, Mrs. Miller, do come in."

Brandon tried to catch Amanda's gaze, but she would not look at him. Instead she turned toward the door, holding it open for his parents.

How much more could he handle?

He had no choice but to continue and find out.

Amanda leaned over the counter and let the breath rush from her. She could do this. She could.

Then why was her face so heated? Her hands clammy? And her shoulders shaking?

Standing up to that man had been one of the hardest things she'd done. But how could she stay silent when he implied that she had… that Samuel was…

She put a hand on her forehead as the room spun. What was she thinking? This was too much.

Why hadn't Brandon spoken for her? For Samuel? His father's words had clearly upset him, but he had not said anything.

Monitoring her breaths, she pulled air in and pushed it out. Soon enough, her vision stabilized, and she felt more grounded.

Why had she told Cook she was not needed this evening? They'd even sent the ranch hands off to Cook and Uncle Owen's house for dinner to give them a bit of privacy with Brandon's newly arrived parents. That was the last thing she wanted now.

The door behind her swung open.

"Need any help?"

She turned.

Brandon stood with the door propped open. His features morphed as he took her in—his brows furrowed and his mouth thinned. "Everything all right?"

Now was not the time. So she nodded. "Just catching my breath."

His features did not soften. Did he not believe her?

She stepped to the stovetop, giving the beans a quick stir. They were ready. Pulling at the oven door, she checked that the roast was done as well.

She grabbed for a couple of towels and pulled the pan from the heat then set it next to the pot of beans.

"Shall I carry the roast into the dining room?"

Amanda spun.

Brandon still stood in the opening between the dining room and kitchen.

What would his parents think if she couldn't manage putting the food on the table herself? At the same time, everyone was already seated and waiting. What was best—getting the food to them quicker or saving face?

She nodded and waved for Brandon to come alongside her and get the larger pan as she dumped beans into a serving dish.

He moved off into the dining room, she a few steps behind.

Focusing on her task, she avoided looking in the direction of Brandon's parents.

"My, this smells wonderful," Mrs. Miller said as Brandon moved aside and toward his chair.

Amanda set her dish on the table and straightened. She met Mrs. Miller's gaze and nodded.

Brandon reached for Amanda's hand and drew her to the seat beside him.

"There are no other courses, I presume?" Mr. Miller looked across the table. How did he maintain such rigid posture?

The hand on hers tightened. But Brandon did not speak.

She closed her eyes. Would he say something into the silence?

After a moment of continued quiet, she pulled her hand free of his strengthening grip with some difficulty.

"No, sir," she choked out, her breath catching. "This is what we have."

"It looks delicious." Mrs. Miller leaned toward Amanda.

Brandon's hand rested on her back.

But she would not tolerate it. She moved away and pulled her chair out, seating herself, most certainly under the scrutiny of her father-in-law.

The chair beside her scraped on the floor, and Brandon moved next to her, sitting as well.

"Shall we return thanks?" Brandon said.

Amanda folded her hands in front of herself, but remained silent.

Brandon lifted a brief prayer of gratitude for the food and for their time together then he was finished.

Food and plates were passed and the meal commenced.

She kept her eyes on her food, willing herself not to look up.

The clattering of the silverware against the plates was the only sound.

Crash!

Amanda jerked her head in the direction of the noise.

Samuel had frozen. He stood, leaning across the table, arms extending the serving dish of beans toward Brandon's father.

Mr. Miller's glass of tea had tipped, spilling all over his plate and the surrounding area. The man's eyes were narrowing even then as they set on poor Samuel, who shrank back.

"Look what you've done, you careless child!" Mr. Miller's volume rose as he spoke.

"Charles," Mrs. Miller inserted, "It was only—"

"Not now." He set upon her for a moment. His face reddened as he stood, towering over Samuel's smaller frame.

Mrs. Miller pulled her outstretched hand back into her lap.

"I…I didn't mean to—" Samuel started, staring up at the looming figure.

"Didn't mean to? What did you mean to do?" the man roared, eyes flashing as he set them once more on Samuel.

Amanda opened her mouth, but nothing came forth. She needed to say something. How could she let this…this ogre speak to her son like this? Over such a simple mistake?

"It's a wonder you're even allowed at the same table." Mr. Miller eased back into his chair, readjusting his jacket. He pulled out a handkerchief and fussed over his shirt.

Samuel dropped the bowl and rushed out of the room.

"Good riddance." Brandon's father glanced around the table. "Is anyone going to clean this up?" He waved his stark white cloth at the growing lake around his plate.

Amanda rose, her chair nearly toppling with the

force at which she took to her feet.

Brandon's fingers wrapped around her wrist.

She afforded him a hard look as she jerked her hand free.

His eyes were wide, his mouth parted. Was he preparing to question her?

"I need to see to my son," she forced out through clenched teeth.

Without waiting for a response, she pushed away from him and took her leave of the room with no further explanation.

Not that anyone in that room deserved one.

Brandon hung his head as he stepped toward his and Amanda's bedroom door. What was he to do? What could he say? After she stormed from the dining room, he had been left with a mess—both the spilled drink and the disaster of his father's ire. Neither had been easy without her.

Still, he didn't want to fight. He was much too worn for that. And there were more tense days to come. For both of them.

Grasping the handle, he pushed the door open and stepped within.

Amanda sat across the room at her vanity. She was already dressed for bed and sat gazing in the mirror as she brushed her hair.

He shut the door.

She paused briefly, but soon resumed her strokes.

Did she not care that he was here? Perhaps he didn't care either. He strode across the room. Sitting on the edge of the bed, he pulled at his boots. "How is Samuel?"

A soft sigh sounded from her direction. "He is all right. Though it took a while to calm him."

His boots now off, Brandon turned to look at his wife. Must she be so beautiful?

Her eyes caught his in the mirror. For a moment, they locked, then she let her gaze fall to her hands.

He gripped the knees of his pants. How could he not go to her?

So he stood. And stepped around their bed, slowly making his way toward her.

He stopped just inches away. Would she pull back from his touch? Should that keep him from reaching out?

Pausing but briefly, he hung his head. But it was for naught. He must take the chance. She needed him. Hadn't he vowed *for better or for worse*?

Laying hands that shook more than they should have on her shoulders, he pulled in a breath.

She startled.

Had he surprised her? Surely not. She must have heard his movements.

Her shoulders trembled. Was she crying?

He massaged her quaking arms as he leaned forward and crouched, pressing a kiss to the top of her head. "I'm sorry."

Were there more words to say? Could he speak them? Those two words had been almost impossible to force out. Not because he didn't wish to, but because of the tightness in his throat.

She shifted, turning and wrapping her arms around his upper body.

Everything in him seemed to drop—the tightness loosened, the heat diffused, and his frustration dissipated. His arms surrounded her.

"I am stronger than this." The words were a bit uneven as they slipped from her lips.

"You don't have to be," he whispered into her ear.

She squeezed his shoulders. "Yes, I do."

He ran a hand through her hair. Silk. "We cannot stand on our own strength. We need each other, remember? And we need God."

Nodding into his neck, she sighed. "I don't know what to say. What to do…"

"I know."

She pulled back, wiping a hand across her face.

He looked into her eyes. They seemed deeper somehow.

"You're right about one thing. I can't do it alone."

Captured by her gaze, he could only nod.

"I need God, yes, but I also need…" She closed her eyes for a moment. When they opened, her mouth was set more firmly, and her eyes were harder. "I needed you."

He furrowed his brows. But when he opened his mouth, it was she who spoke.

"I know this must be incredibly difficult for you, but I needed you to speak for me. For Samuel."

His face fell. And he looked to the ground.

"Why didn't you? Why did you let your father say those things?"

Silence fell between them for a moment.

He lifted his eyes to meet hers. "You must know, Amanda, that I would never let *anyone*, including my father…especially my father, believe those things about you. Or Samuel. I was just so…angry…that I couldn't speak."

Her brows tilted upward while her lips formed a soft arch.

Taking her hands in his, he lifted them to his chest. "Surely you know that much about me by now." Did she not? Why must he convince her? Did she trust him so little? After everything they had been through?

She pressed her hands flat on his chest. Then laid her head there as well. "I do."

He let out a long breath and embraced her. Yet he could not shake the nagging feeling that all was not well between them.

Amanda opened her eyes. She found herself securely wrapped by her husband's arm and leaning against his broad chest.

She ran a hand over his muscled frame until her fingers found his heartbeat. How she loved that simple rhythmic pounding—the assurance of life and health.

Looking at his eyes, still closed, she moved closer and laid her head over where his heart pounded.

His arms moved around her, and he pressed a kiss into her hair. "Good morning."

She smiled. It had not been her intention to wake him, but it was not uncommon for him find her in this position. "Good morning."

"How am I this morning?"

His chest vibrated as he spoke. It soothed her. "Quite well." She ran her fingertips across his upper body. "Your heart is strong and sure."

"Because of you," he whispered.

Turning her head, she looked at him. Must he be so sweet? Where did he come up with such endearing words?

Shifting, he brought his lips to hers.

The kiss was gentle and full of promise. And she could only guess what would come of it. But she had a pretty good idea.

He broke off their contact and traced her features with a fingertip.

As much as she longed to let him continue his ministrations, she could not. She caught his hand, pressed a kiss to his finger, and rolled away.

"Wait a minute," he said, reaching for her.

"You forget yourself. I have to make breakfast

for our guests." She arched a brow.

His hand fell back to the bed, and he groaned.

She moved to her trunk and rummaged through the dresses, finally selecting one for the day.

As she pulled at the strings of her laced up nightdress, a whoosh and the padding of feet across the floor warned her of his presence before his arms around her midsection did.

"Just a little while longer," he pled, his lips on her neck.

He could be very convincing. But the image of his father, and the man's words came back to her.

She stiffened. "No. I need to get everything ready."

He loosened his grip and stepped back. "All right, but only if you promise me that later, we'll—"

She put a hand to the side of his face. "Perhaps."

Nodding, his eyes sparkled. All he needed was the promise of a possibility. He then turned to his own preparations for the day, and she swapped her nightdress for her favorite blue gingham dress.

It wasn't long until she was putting the finishing touches on her hair.

"See you in an hour?" Brandon encircled her again with his arms.

"An hour." How would she manage his parents without him for so long? Couldn't he skip his morning chores? Still she set her expression and offered him a smile. She could do this. She would.

Stepping through the hall, she was careful not to

make any noise. She was thankful Louise was a sound sleeper. It would be a good thirty minutes before she arose.

As she neared the kitchen door, voices from within, muffled by the door, gave her pause. Were she and Brandon not the only ones awake in the house? Who could it be?

She waited for a handful of moments outside the kitchen door, trying to determine who traipsed about her kitchen. Then chided herself for doing so. Nothing would be gained from standing here and wondering.

So, she pushed the door open and stepped in.

"Mrs. Amanda," Cook exclaimed. "We were starting to think you would never get up." There was a twinkle in the woman's eye.

Cook? But she didn't get here until after—

"Good morning," Mrs. Miller stepped toward Amanda. She held Louise. "The little Miss and I were just getting better acquainted. How are you this morning?"

"I...I am well." Could she hide her confusion or was it written across her features?

Mrs. Miller touched her arm. "Don't worry, dear. I'm an early riser. Always have been. And Cook was just keeping me company. Then this little darling decided she was finished sleeping." Brandon's mother bounced Louise on her hip.

"I'm sure them ranch hands gonna think Mr. Brandon done abandoned them for sure." Cook winked at Amanda.

Her face warmed. Why, she was not certain. It wasn't as if they had been doing anything. What time was it? Had they overslept? Or was everyone else early?

"H-how are you this morning, Mrs. Miller?" Amanda regained enough of her mind to ask.

"Well enough." The woman smiled.

Amanda saw the growing moisture on Mrs. Miller's shoulder. Louise was drooling on her fine dress! "Mrs. Miller, your dress! I am so sorry. I fear Louise may be getting teeth. Do you need me to take her?"

"No. It's all right. I just adore young ones!" Mrs. Miller hugged Louise to herself. "I think we'll go find some blocks to explore."

With that, Mrs. Miller moved off in the direction of the dining room.

As she exited, Amanda turned to Cook. "What time is it?" She pushed out through clenched teeth.

"It's might near six o'clock."

Amanda wanted for somewhere to sit. Six o'clock! How could she and Brandon have slept in so late?

"Don't you go faintin' on me now." Cook jerked on her arm. "It's not the worst thing in the world."

Her hand landed on Cook's. "You don't understand. You're not under Mr. Miller's eyeglass. He —"

"Is not up yet."

Amanda searched for the words to describe just

how horrible Mr. Miller had been without actually saying he had been horrible. What if he were to hear?

Wait.

What had Cook said?

"He's not up yet?"

"Nope. Haven't seen nor heard as much as a peep from him."

Amanda chewed on her lip. What should she make of that?

Cook turned and moved away toward the stove, stirring this and that.

Breakfast.

She had already forgotten they were to be making breakfast. Was she so useless?

After grabbing her apron, she made quick work of tying it. "How can I help?"

Cook directed her toward the biscuits, and they spent the better part of the next hour getting the details of the meal assembled and perfected.

As Amanda prepared the table, Cook called the men in.

Mrs. Miller brought Louise to the dining room while Brandon, Cutie, Dan, and Slim filed in and found their places around the table. Samuel rushed in behind them. Had he been out doing chores with the men? He should be getting ready for school.

One chair remained empty.

Mr. Miller's seat.

All eyes shifted between Brandon and Mrs. Miller. Who would speak? Should they wait?

After some moments, Mrs. Miller seemed to become aware of the trouble. "It is not uncommon for Mr. Miller to…linger in his room these days. We should eat without him. He will eat when he is ready."

"When he is ready?" Brandon said. "He does not wish to eat with us?"

Mrs. Miller appeared stricken. Almost as if she had been slapped. "It is not that. He is just…still abed."

"Sleeping? He has overslept? That is why he will not eat with us? Because he wishes to sleep?"

Amanda laid a hand on Brandon's arm. Could she keep him from becoming more agitated? Would he calm?

"Perhaps he is just tired from his long trip." Amanda caught Brandon's eyes. "It does not mean that he intends offense."

"Yes," Mrs. Miller said, meeting Amanda's gaze, and then Brandon's. "He certainly does not mean to offend."

The room became silent and Brandon's gaze swept from Amanda's to his mother's and back again.

"I suppose that can be true." He leaned toward his plate. "Let us return grace."

Amanda and Mrs. Miller exchanged a glance, and Amanda did not miss the gratitude in her mother-in-law's eyes.

CHAPTER THREE

Christmas Tree Trials

THE WAGON JOSTLED Brandon as it moved along the rocky hillside. But instead of complaints from the passenger seat, the bumps brought giggles.

Samuel couldn't get enough of the scenery, of the horses, of being out in the midst of the wilds of Arizona. And, could it be, he simply enjoyed being with Brandon?

Brandon had handed the reins to the boy about two miles back, and he was rather impressed with the young man's ability to manage the animals.

"That's it. Just keep a firm grip." Brandon reached a hand out toward Samuel's. "Not too tight. They'll think you want them to stop."

Sure enough, the horses began to slow.

With Brandon's help, Samuel let some slack in the reins, but only just enough.

"There. That's it." Brandon pulled his hand back and let Samuel have full command again.

"Look, Pa!" Samuel glanced at him. "I'm doing it!"

"You sure are." Brandon's heart warmed every time Samuel called him 'Pa.' They had been through much. And the journey to where they were now had not been easy. But the fight had been well worth it.

Samuel's attention was on the horses once more.

Brandon laid an arm behind him on the bench and used that hand to pat his shoulder. "You're a natural."

Samuel's toothy grin widened.

And Brandon's chest expanded. How could it be that this young boy could make him feel so proud? So accomplished? Was this what all fathers felt?

What was it like for Jed? Was he proud of Samuel? He hoped that Samuel had fond memories of his real father. More so than Brandon.

He frowned. While it was true there was tension between him and his father, there was no reason he needed to bring it into this moment. Today was for him and Samuel. His father had stolen enough of this holiday season from them.

The man continued to pick and plague his family. These last few days had been nothing but increasing tension between them and Father. And between him and Amanda for his inability to speak up to his father. What kept him from doing so? Some sense of loyalty? Of respect? Hadn't he let those things go long ago?

Hadn't he turned away from the man's desires for him? Of Father's plans? Challenged his father to disown him even?

How then was he now too timid to speak up to the man?

It was nonsense.

"I think our tree is over there." Samuel pointed off to the right.

Sure enough, there was a fine grouping of conifer evergreens.

"Let's steer the horses closer and give them the slow down signal."

Samuel nodded.

Brandon scooted closer to him and wrapped his arms around the boy, setting his hands on the youngster's arms.

Pulling the reins hard right, Samuel urged the horses to turn.

"Whoa there, not so much."

Samuel eased his turn, but the horses did not correct themselves accordingly. They continued in their hard right turn.

"Pa!"

"Don't panic," Brandon said calmly. "What do you think might work?"

Samuel pulled the reins to the left, putting just

enough pressure to adjust the horse's direction. When they were headed toward the targeted area, Samuel tightened his pull to the right, so that he was pulling both with equal force. And the horses slowed to a stop.

"Great work."

"Did I do right?" Samuel looked up at Brandon with eyes as big as tea saucers.

"Yes." Brandon jerked the brim of Samuel's hat. "You did right."

Then there was that smile again.

Endearing.

It reminded him of Amanda.

Amanda.

If only this tension with his father wasn't making their time troubled also…if only there were a way to let her know he still cherished her more than all that.

The Christmas dance! He had almost forgotten.

It was to be in two days. He must ask her tonight. After they had put up the tree. That's when he would do it. This would be just the thing for them to get away and spend time just the two of them.

"Pa?"

Brandon turned.

Samuel still looked at him, his eyebrows furrowed and his mouth askance.

"Sorry, little man. I was just thinking about something I need to ask your Ma."

"Oh?"

"Adult stuff."

"Oh." Samuel's face fell.

"I'll tell you about it when you're older."

Samuel's mouth twisted.

Brandon chuckled. "Come on, that tree isn't going to cut itself." He worked his way to the ground and reached up for Samuel, only to discover that the boy had similarly used the bench and large front wheel to ease his way down.

Reaching into the wagon bed, Brandon grabbed his axe and waved for Samuel to follow. They made their way to the trees. After a close inspection, they chose a moderately sized conifer that was thicker than the others.

Brandon had Samuel stand back several feet while he chopped it down, and together they dragged it to the wagon as they shared their favorite things about the Christmas season.

With some difficulty, they managed to get the tree into the wagon and commenced to tying the tree down just enough so it wouldn't slide out during the trip home.

"Last knot," Brandon told Samuel. "Probably the most important."

Samuel nodded.

"So, watch me."

The boy moved closer to Brandon. "Ow!"

"What is it?" Was he hurt? How?

Samuel stepped back and Brandon saw what was amiss. The axe lay between them and he must have stepped against the metal head.

"Are you hurt?" Brandon leaned toward the boy. "Let me take a look."

"I think I'm all right." Samuel rubbed at his shin.

Brandon lifted Samuel's pant leg and glanced at the skin, rubbing a hand along the area to confirm nothing had been injured. No skin was broken and there were no discernible bumps or reddened areas. "I think you're right. I don't see anything."

Samuel nodded.

"How about for good measure, I put this in the cart where I should have put it to begin with?"

"Can I?" Samuel picked up the axe. It was apparent that he could hardly lift it, much less throw it.

Brandon thought for a moment. What could it hurt? The boy was tall enough to fling it into the bed of the cart without missing. Still, there was the slight chance he could hit the side and the axe would bounce back and hit one of them.

Perhaps they could do it together.

"All right. But don't throw it. Toss it like this." Brandon got behind him, moved them both closer to the wagon, and showed him how to hold the axe with both hands and scoop it upward.

And together they flung it toward the bed of the cart.

It landed with a loud thud.

One of the horses reared.

Spooked.

It jerked forward.

There was no time.

Brandon shoved Samuel away from the cart.

But as Brandon attempted to leap to safety, he realized he couldn't move, and pain tore through his right foot.

He cried out.

His foot had been pinned under the wheel as it moved forward.

Samuel moved toward him.

"No!" Brandon held out a hand to Samuel. Would that stop him?

The boy froze, wide-eyed as the horses continued to gain speed as they moved onward.

Brandon curled into a fetal position as he reached for his injured foot. Was it broken?

It hurt. It throbbed.

Dare he remove his boot? Would that make it worse? Would that scare Samuel?

The boy was by his side in the next moment. "Pa! Are you all right?"

Brandon clenched his teeth and put an arm around Samuel. "I'm going to be fine." He met Samuel's eyes. It was clear the boy did not believe him. "I'm more worried about the horses."

Samuel pointed northward. "They headed that way."

Brandon's eyes followed where Samuel indicated. The pair were going as fast as possible.

Two things he knew: they would never catch them, and the tree would not survive the trip. If the horses were indeed headed back to the ranch.

Brandon looked to his foot. They would have to search for help or hobble home. But one thing was certain: unless they found help quickly, they'd be spending the night out in wilds of Arizona.

Was it that time already? Time for holiday cookies and baked goods? The Christmas season seemed to have snuck up.

Amanda reached for a rolling pin. Hadn't she been preparing for Christmas? Yes, her home was decorated. Then where was her holiday cheer? Gone. Perhaps when *he* had come into their lives.

And disrupted everything.

It was just awful that she had such thoughts. Terrible.

Lord, Give me peace. Give me grace for this man, my husband's father. Your word says that we are to love our enemies and pray for those who persecute us. Well, he is the closest thing to an enemy I have, and I have never felt so persecuted as I do when he talks down to me. So, I lift him up to you. Whatever is making him so bitter, so mean...so...

"I hope I'm not disturbing you."

Amanda let out a cry as she spun, pin raised above her head, prepared to defend herself.

Mrs. Miller shrunk back.

"Dear Lord." Amanda put a hand to her chest.

Could she calm the pounding within? "I didn't know you were there."

"I'm sorry." Mrs. Miller straightened. "I didn't mean to startle you so."

Amanda lowered the rolling pin. "I was just... my mind was elsewhere."

"As I could see." The older woman's mouth twinged into a half-smile. "Nothing serious, I hope."

"No." Amanda's face warmed. Could her mother-in-law see into her mind? Discern her thoughts? "Just thinking, praying, and working on cookies."

"Cookies?" Mrs. Miller stepped to the counter alongside Amanda. "One of my favorite things! What are they? Sugar? Chocolate chip? Oh, please tell me they are sugar!"

"Yes. They are...Brandon's favorite." They said the last two words in unison.

Then Mrs. Miller giggled. "How could I forget? He was always stealing cookies off the plate before they'd had time to cool."

Amanda smiled. "He still does that."

Mrs. Miller sighed. "It's nice to know that some things don't change." She looked off into the distance. There was a sadness in her eyes that Amanda didn't quite understand.

"Would you like to help?"

"Me?"

Amanda nodded.

"Are you certain I won't be in the way?"

"Of course not. I need an extra hand. Samuel

used to help with decorating the cookies. But now, he doesn't care to. So, it's left up to me until Louise is old enough."

Mrs. Miller looked at Amanda, a twinkle in her eye as she bit at her lip. It was apparent she truly wanted to help.

"Please." Amanda stepped to the side. "Would you rather roll or cut?"

"Could I cut?"

"Yes. I'll be finished rolling it out in a minute." Amanda turned back toward the mound of dough that was only half flattened. As she rolled, she tried to think of how she might engage the woman in conversation.

"I have been wanting to find time alone with you," Mrs. Miller said.

"Oh?" Should she be nervous? What could the woman need to say to her?

"Yes. I see the way my son looks at you."

Oh no. Here it comes. She and Brandon hadn't exactly been on good terms lately. How could she tell her mother-in-law that it was her husband who brought out the worst in her?

"And you make him so happy."

Amanda stopped rolling and looked at the older woman.

"You don't know what that does to a mother's heart. Especially one that has hurt for her son for so long. Not knowing how he is or what is happening to him. But now I know he has you. And you are good for him."

How could she respond to that? Her mouth moved, but no sound came out.

Mrs. Miller put a hand on her shoulder. "I know. And I know my husband may not be the easiest to get along with. Or the most generous with his words."

That was an understatement.

The woman's eyes glistened. "But he is a good man. And he, too, just wants the best for Brandon."

Amanda wanted to believe that. Yet she struggled to.

"Oh my goodness!" Mrs. Miller looked at the dough. "You have it all ready, and I am remiss in my part of the task." She picked up the cookie cutters and sliced through the dough cleanly, making what few shapes they had.

Watching her mother-in-law at work gave Amanda an opportunity to reflect on her words. What if they were misunderstanding Mr. Miller? Was it possible there was more to him? Her mind reran his comments and reactions. It just didn't seem possible.

"Here, now I'll roll it out and let you cut." Mrs. Miller gathered the remaining dough into a ball and rolled it out in half the time it had taken Amanda.

Then Amanda worked the cutters.

They chatted about more mundane things and even laughed. The time passed more pleasantly than Amanda could have hoped.

Once the cookies were in the oven and they had washed everything, they sat at the dining table with cups of coffee.

"You must come to Richmond," Mrs. Miller said. "I would enjoy showing you off."

"Oh, I don't know." Amanda spread her hands on the table. "Ranch life doesn't give much time for travel. But you are welcome to visit whenever you would like." She remembered that Mr. Miller would come with her and coughed to cover up a sudden choke.

"Are you well, dear?" Mrs. Miller reached across the table to grasp her hand.

"Yes. Just sipped too fast."

Mrs. Miller nodded and took a sip of coffee before setting her cup down and turning it. Her eyes on the coffee. "I have a confession to make."

Amanda's brows shot up, but she kept her silence.

"I was a little…concerned. About you." Mrs. Miller's gaze met hers. "Before we came." The words rushed from the woman as she clasped Amanda's hand once again. "I am so pleased with my son's choice of wife. Truly, I am. But, before we came, I wondered—worried, really—how well we might be received."

Mrs. Miller paused.

Amanda swallowed. What should she think of this? Wasn't it only natural for a mother to be concerned about a new wife she had never met?

"So, I wrote to Owen and Cook, asking after you."

The breath Amanda released could not be disguised.

Mrs. Miller's brows drooped. Was she

confused? Concerned?

Leaning over her coffee, Amanda smiled. "I have a confession of my own."

One of the older woman's brows shot up.

"I already knew about that letter."

"But I thought—"

"I didn't know until after we received your letter. Cook did keep your secret. But she confided the existence of the letter. Though, she did not mention the contents."

Mrs. Miller nodded. Her gaze fell to her cup once more.

"I am glad you came." Amanda surprised herself by saying, "It is good for Brandon to see you, if nothing else. That is why I must insist you come again. As often as you can."

"This trip was rather…difficult. I…don't think we'll be able to make another before…"

Her silence dragged out.

"Before what?"

Mrs. Miller's eyes watered, and she waved a hand between them. "It's nothing. We are just of such an age, you see? I…excuse me." She stood and moved out of the room quicker than Amanda would have thought possible.

What was going on?

Lying on his back, Brandon bit the inside of his cheek

to keep from swearing. His right foot hurt, yes, but it was the situation that vexed him the most. Here he was, injured, far away from the ranch, and charged with caring for Samuel.

How he wished that all three of these challenges were not present. If but one of them had not been, he would not be in such a fix. But it was pointless to hope for things to be different. They were not.

Pulling his hand from over his eyes, he looked at Samuel. The boy's gaze was already upon him. Why did he have to seem so trusting? So certain Brandon would save the day? That did nothing to ease Brandon's guilt.

Enough.

He had lain here and pitied himself long enough. It was time for action.

First—could he walk? Rising into a seated position, he glanced about. Was there a branch or something similar nearby he might use as a crutch?

Nothing stuck out.

He turned to Samuel and took a deep breath. It was time to be honest.

"I don't know how bad my foot is."

Samuel nodded, his eyes widening.

"I want to try to put weight on it." Brandon watched as Samuel's features paled slightly.

Could Samuel do this? He would have to.

"I'm afraid I'll need to lean on you."

The boy nodded again. His jaw became set. "Just tell me what to do."

Brandon offered him a smile, encouraged that Samuel would persevere. He motioned for the boy to come around to his right.

Samuel obeyed, crouching next to Brandon on that side.

Wrapping an arm around Samuel's shoulders, he rose, putting as much weight as he could onto his left arm and leg as he did so.

Once he was upright, he tested his right foot—taking a step while allowing some of his weight to rest on Samuel.

Pain shot through him. But his leg did not give way.

A good sign he had not broken anything. Still, he would not be able to walk far like this. He was too heavy for Samuel to bear even a portion of his weight for long, and he didn't know how long he could withstand the pain before passing out. Or what damage he would do by pushing through.

"I'll go for help." Samuel's voice was small, but steady.

Was he serious? They were quite a distance from any homesteads. And if Samuel should be injured, or lost…

He couldn't risk it.

"I think it's best if we stick together."

Samuel hung his head.

"I don't think I can manage without you." Brandon smiled at him. "You've got to keep me company."

"But you can't walk." When Samuel looked at Brandon, his features were solemn. Did he know the seriousness of the situation?

"It's all right. As long as we're together, we'll be okay. We'll think of something. Maybe we can make it to the road."

Samuel frowned. His eyes were sad. Was he so doubtful? Had he guessed what Brandon knew? That he could not hold Brandon's weight for more than a couple of steps and that Brandon was not able to put that weight on his injured foot?

"If only there was a branch…" Brandon scanned the area again.

"A branch?" Had that thought not occurred to him?

"Yeah. Do you see a branch large enough to be a crutch?"

"No. But I bet I can find one." Samuel's gaze drifted toward the grouping of evergreen trees.

Brandon's eyes followed. "Yes. I bet you could." Turning to Samuel, hope sparking anew, he released the boy's shoulder and eased back down to the ground. "Go."

Samuel took off into the trees.

And Brandon prayed his errand would prove successful. If not, they may be out of safe options. It would be up to him to pick the best of the bad choices available.

Amanda eased back in her chair. She had less time for peace these days. With her, home was always filled with laughter…and Brandon's father. And then her little Louise always needed something. But having just put the little one down for a nap, Amanda had earned herself some quiet.

She watched the cattle in the far off pastures as they grazed and the ranch hands as they moved about between the fields, the cows, and the barn. Life was full, but simple. Just as she preferred.

As she gazed across the beautiful landscape, she noted what a lovely picture the afternoon sun made in the clouded sky. So nice, so pleasant, so…

Afternoon?

How had she missed it?

Had she been so distracted by Louise, and cookies, and Brandon's mother that she didn't notice?

Brandon and Samuel had not returned.

And it was long past the time they should have. Should she be worried?

Perhaps they had returned and went back to work?

There was one way to find out.

She rose and hurried toward the field. As she approached Dan, he spotted her and closed the distance between them before halting his horse.

"Good afternoon, ma'am. Is there something I

can do for ya?"

"Good afternoon. I wondered if Brandon and Samuel had returned with the Christmas tree."

Dan shook his head. "Not that I'm aware of."

She should let it go, but something didn't set right about it. Something in the pit of her stomach. It would likely come to naught, but she didn't care. "Could you ask Cutie and Slim if they've seen them?"

His eyebrow rose slightly. "Sure thing." He turned his horse back the direction he had come and set off after his cohorts.

But she was quite certain she would not be able to just wait. So, she made her way into the barn to check the stalls. Perhaps she might spy if the horses were back.

A quick walk through the barn yielded nothing. The horses were not returned. But as she paused by the far side of the barn, she heard something. Didn't she? It was there, and then gone.

She halted her movements and tilted her head.

Yes, there it was again. A snorting sound.

It came from the back side of the barn.

Tiptoeing in that direction, she slipped out the back door. There, on the small hillside, a few feet away, stood Brandon's cart and two horses, munching away.

What had happened? Had Brandon come back and not stabled the horses? That didn't make sense.

She moved toward the horses, careful to take slow steps.

At last, she reached the closest horse and

grasped its bridle. The horse did not so much as blink at her. Just kept munching. She gave its neck a good pat and ran her hand along its body as she moved toward its rear.

Now she could see into the bed of the cart—remnants of rope and pieces of tree were all that remained.

What? It made no sense.

Where were her husband and son?

"Mrs. Miller?" a voice called from the barn.

She moved to the horse's head again and grabbed for the reins. "I'm out back!"

The door of the barn opened, and Dan stuck his head out.

"Isn't that—?"

"Yes—the cart and horses Brandon and Samuel took. Have Cutie or Slim seen them?" Her pitch rose. Was she fooling herself? Working to keep the truth from herself?

Dan stepped closer. "No, ma'am. They haven't returned."

"Then…" Her voice trailed off.

He nodded. "They are out there—somewhere—without a way back home."

She dropped the reins as her hands flew to her mouth. "What are we going to do?"

"You aren't going to do anything." Dan's voice was firm. "Cutie, Slim, and I are going to find them."

"But, I want to help. I can ride—"

"It would be best if you wait here. What if they

came back and we were all out looking?"

She nodded but couldn't form words.

"Think about what Mr. Miller would want. Wouldn't he want you to stay here? To look after Miss Louise and his parents."

That was true. "All right. I'll stay."

Dan sighed.

"But," she said, glaring at him. "I won't wait here forever. If you do not bring them back in two hours, I'm riding out."

He opened his mouth.

"*Two* hours."

Hands on hips, he didn't seem ready to concede.

"Your time is wasting."

His eyes widened. He turned, hesitantly, and moved off toward the south pasture.

As he rounded the corner of the barn, Amanda collapsed onto her knees.

Please, God, please keep them safe.

CHAPTER FOUR

The Truth

BRANDON HOBBLED UP the incline. If they ever made it home, it would be months before he agreed to hitch those horses for so much as a country drive.

But he would find a way to thank Samuel. That was for certain. The boy kept to his side. Not that he could do much, still he lingered near the injured foot, preparing to be needed.

Clenching his teeth as they went, Brandon refused to let loose any noise, any sign that he struggled against such pain. But if Samuel was half as smart as Brandon thought him to be, he already guessed. Still, Brandon did not wish to burden him with the reminder.

Besides, there was nothing he could do.

The sun continued to move across the sky. How long until it would set? They'd have no choice but to build a makeshift shelter. It would not be safe to remain in the open. Not with the night dwelling wildlife in search of a meal.

With naught but this branch as a weapon, they were easy prey.

This, too, he kept to himself.

"We'll be home in time for cookies," Brandon grunted between gasps.

"Yeah." Samuel did not so much as look in Brandon's direction. Did he not believe Brandon?

Neither should he.

Not if he had any sense.

Though their situation may be grim, there was no reason Brandon needed to speak of it. That would not serve either of them. And so, they moved in their offbeat rhythm in the general direction of the main road.

Was it best he not speak at all? Perhaps. Keeping his eyes on the ground and concentrating on his movements, the journey became as quiet as it was arduous.

Over and over, Brandon set the branch-turned-crutch onto the ground, leaning heavily upon it.

Snap!

It gave way under his weight.

He fell, as there was no longer anything supporting him. As he crumpled, he became somewhat aware of Samuel's attempt to hold him up.

Brandon fought through the pain to take in his surroundings.

Samuel was under him, groaning.

He jerked and half-rolled, relieving the child of his weight. "Samuel! Are you well?" His words came in gasps.

The boy had curled into a ball.

Brandon shook his head. What could clear this fog? He reached a hand out to touch the youngster's back. "Are you hurt?"

Samuel shook his head, but would not look at him or release the smaller limbs from his tight fetal position.

What happened? Brandon searched for the culprit—his branch.

The bottom portion of the makeshift crutch still stuck in the ground. A hole. It must have found a hole. And the force had cracked it in two; there was nothing to be done.

Of all the bad luck.

He drew his hand into a fist and raised it. Without a suitable target for his anger, the ground would do nicely,. But he caught Samuel's form in the corner of his eye. While it may make him feel a little better, it might only distress the boy more.

Gritting his teeth, Brandon scooted closer to the shaking bundle.

Stretching his arms forth, he pulled Samuel closer until he had the child in his embrace, huddled against his chest.

"It's all right, son. We'll be okay."

He rubbed a hand through Samuel's hair.

"We can handle anything. As long as we're together, right?"

Samuel's trembling calmed.

The time for a decision had come. Would they try to journey further? How could Brandon go even one more step without assistance? Should he send Samuel after another branch? Perhaps Samuel could go after help? Or maybe they might make a shelter and sit out the night. Amanda and the ranch hands would be looking for them come dawn. Surely they'd be found by midday.

If they survived the night.

They would.

They had to.

God, keep us safe!

Brandon leaned his head down, trying to catch Samuel's eyes.

And thunder rumbled in the distance.

One more challenge they didn't need.

Or could it be…?

Tears stung Amanda's eyes as she watched the horizon for any sign of return. From any of the men.

Where were they? What had happened? Were they in some sort of danger? As the night closed in, the danger increased.

The two hours she had given Dan had come and gone. Time for her to saddle up and go in search of her husband and son.

She turned and stepped into the house. Brandon's mother sat in the great room with Louise. But the woman's eyes settled on Amanda the moment she entered.

"Is there news?"

"No." Amanda kept her gaze steady and swallowed against the tightness in her throat.

Even across the room, she saw the older woman's tears forming.

"It is time for me to join the search."

Mrs. Miller gripped Louise and rose, a little unsteadily. "You, dear?"

"Yes."

"Is that safe?"

While Amanda wanted to be upset at the woman's lack of faith, the question came from a place of concern.

"I cannot stay here and do nothing. Not while my…" her voice broke.

Mrs. Miller nodded and crossed the space until she laid a hand on Amanda's shoulder. "I will pray."

A tear escaped, sliding down Amanda's face. She wiped at it. "Thank you."

Amanda turned, making her way onto the porch, intent on her mission.

But a sound in the distance drew her.

There. On the path. Two riders.

The dimness prevented her from discerning anything else.

Were the ranch hands returning with news? Or with nothing? Would they give up for the night and resume in the morning? They may try and insist she do the same, but they would not succeed.

She stepped off the porch and onto the firm ground. Long strides carried her to intercept the men.

As they neared, their outlines became clearer. The horses each bore two riders. Could it be?

Picking up her skirt, she rushed toward them.

The riders slowed as they closed in upon her.

Dan and Cutie had indeed found them.

Brandon and Samuel were on their horses.

Her hand flew to her mouth as she let out a cry.

Dan dismounted and assisted Brandon's somewhat clumsy drop to the ground. Was something amiss?

She didn't care. Closing the distance in a moment, she wrapped her arms around him.

He let out a sound as the air rushed from him. But his arms enclosed her all the same, and his lips pressed into her hair.

"I thought…" Her tears overcame her, and she couldn't finish.

"Shhh," he whispered. "We're together again. There is no need."

Another body, smaller, slammed into her.

She pulled away from Brandon's chest only far enough to look down.

Samuel.

Falling to her knees, she enveloped him. And the tears flowed.

When at last she released Samuel, she looked at her husband. He had one arm around Dan. She quirked an eyebrow and rose, keeping a hand on Samuel's. "What is the matter?"

"It is a bit of a story. But the short of it is that I have injured my foot. I don't think it is broken, but it could use some tending to."

She looked back at Samuel. Was he also injured? Her lips parted.

"Samuel is well enough," Brandon said before she could ask. "Just a little worn out. He was brave." Reaching forth, Brandon tousled his hair.

Amanda afforded her son a smile. Then she shifted her focus toward more immediate matters. "Let's get you into the house so I can have a better look at that foot." She turned toward the homestead and indicated Dan should follow.

With great effort, they got Brandon up the stairs and into the house.

Mrs. Miller sat in the great room, watching Louise on the floor. Her gaze set on the men and Amanda as they entered. "Praise the Lord Almighty!"

Amanda was intent on her task and had no time for distractions. She motioned for Dan to bring Brandon around to another chair. As Dan eased his boss into the chair, Amanda brought a lantern closer, handing it to Dan.

"What is this? Is something amiss?" Mrs. Miller scooped up Louise and backed away.

"All is well," Brandon said. "I have some sort of minor injury to my foot."

Amanda focused on removing Brandon's boot with care, so as not to cause him more pain. She did not see the woman's reaction, but she heard Mrs. Miller's intake of breath.

"Mother, please." Brandon's full attention was on Mrs. Miller. "Do not worry yourself."

Perhaps with his self-imposed distraction, she could better work off this boot. It was proving difficult. Was his foot swollen?

"What's this?" A loud voice boomed.

Amanda knew that voice—Mr. Miller. Had they disturbed his rest?

"Your son has been found," Mrs. Miller said. "But he is injured." It became clear in her voice that she had lost control of her emotions.

"Of all the…" Mr. Miller started. "Can he not manage a simple task without injuring himself and causing a ruckus among his workmen?"

Amanda stole a glance at her husband.

His features were tight.

"I told you this was not the place for you. Do you still not see that you are not cut out for this ranching business? This life?"

"Not cut out for this life?" Brandon seethed through clenched teeth.

Would he explode now? Tell his father exactly

what he thought? What would come of it?

Amanda set a hand on his knee and squeezed it.

He looked at her.

Could she calm him? How? No good would come from him verbally sparring with his father right now. This was not the moment. Not with her children in the room.

"I think Louise may be ready to go down." Amanda shifted her gaze to Mrs. Miller.

The older woman seemed reluctant to tear her eyes from her husband and son. But she did. "What? Yes, of course."

When she looked to Brandon, Amanda was pleased to see him draw in several deep breaths.

"Samuel, can you help Mr. Cutie put away the horses?"

"I want to stay with you and Pa."

Amanda's gaze cut to him. "I need you to obey."

He dropped his head. "Yes, Ma." And he sauntered out of the room.

"In my day, boys did not talk back to their parents." Mr. Miller crossed his arms over his chest. How could he manage that with his chest puffed out so?

Brandon closed his eyes and drew in another deep breath.

Without turning from Brandon's injury, Amanda spoke. "Mr. Miller, I mean no disrespect. But, if you're not going to help, I need to ask you to step out." Amanda kept her voice even.

The man's eyes widened. "And I—"

"Step out!" Brandon bit, his gaze hard on his father.

Mr. Miller narrowed his eyes but, after a few moments, turned and took his leave of the great room.

Amanda sought Brandon's eyes, but he closed them and leaned his head back on the chair. She wanted to have that connection with him, but it would not be. So, she refocused on his boot.

And, soon after, the house was filled with Brandon's stifled screams of pain.

The room was dark. Where was he? Brandon looked from side to side. His bedroom. How had he gotten here? He searched his memory.

The Christmas tree…the horse and cart incident…his foot. These things he remembered quite clearly. And he and Samuel were stranded. Then Samuel had waved down a rider passing nearby—Cutie. They were rescued.

His mind continued to piece together the details of their return home and the brief interaction with his father. And how Amanda had stayed his desire to respond. Why?

He turned to his wife.

She shifted in her sleep, turning toward him. After some moments, her eyes opened.

"Brandon?" She leaned up on an elbow. "Are you well?"

He nodded.

"Are you in pain?" Her eyes ran along his body.

Should he tell her the truth? What purpose would that serve? Then again, what use was a lie? "A bit. It isn't bad."

Her features drooped. "We should have gone for the doctor."

"You did a fine job."

She met his gaze again. "But I am not trained, I'm—"

He reached out and cupped her face. "You did what you could. We can call for the doctor tomorrow if need be."

Leaning into his hand, she turned to press a kiss to his palm. Tears brimmed, catching the bit of moonlight coming in through the window.

"What is it?"

"I…I was so scared."

With careful movements, so as not to disturb his injury, he gathered her in his arms and pulled her to his chest.

She settled against him, nuzzling into the space just below his neck, so that his chin rested on her silken locks.

"I'm just sorry I didn't get you that Christmas tree," he said. Would a joke lighten the somber mood?

"Oh, that tree isn't worth so much as it nearly cost."

Her tears wet his skin. Perhaps his joke was ill timed. "Don't you know by now, my darling? I will always come back to you."

She buried her face in his chest, and her body shook.

What had he said? He'd meant to reassure her. Stroking hair that gleamed in the gentle light, he attempted to soothe her.

"You…you can't promise that." Her voice had more volume than he expected.

How could he respond? She had him caught. It had been a foolish thing to say. Bringing a hand up, winding its way through her tresses, he pressed her ever nearer. "No, I cannot."

All was silent but for her sniffling.

"But we are not without hope." He pushed the stray hair from her face and wiped at her tears.

Her whimpers stopped.

"We must trust that God has a plan. That He will not take me one day sooner than He is ready."

She drew in a ragged breath and let it out, equally as broken. "And what if I am not ready when He is?"

He trailed the back of his hand along her upper arm. "Then His grace will be sufficient."

Her hands on his shirt loosened. What had he expected? More tears?

"I fear my faith is too small."

He tipped her head toward his with a finger on her chin. "Now that, I do not believe."

With eyes that were wide, she searched his soul. Would she be wanting? Or would she come away refreshed? He had to find strength for her. The kind that did not come from him alone.

Father, fill me anew.

"Remember," he said as he ran fingers through the length of her hair. "Faith as small as a mustard seed is all that is needed to move mountains."

Though his lips spread, hers did not. Nor did her eyes cease their wide-eyed stare. How was he to comfort her? To assure her?

A breath passed between them. And her lids lowered. They remained such for so long, Brandon thought perhaps she had returned to sleep. If not that she still held to his nightshirt.

He covered one of her hands, pulling it free from the cloth.

Then her eyes were upon him once again, her pupils constricting in the dimness.

"Come, my love," he soothed. "You are tired."

"Tired?" The word fell from her mouth before she bit at the lower, trembling lip. "I am weary."

His forehead tightened as his brows furrowed.

Her eyes glistened, but no tears fell. Had they dried up, all spent?

"Do you not see it?" Those hazel orbs vanished behind long lashes.

"See what?"

"That I have reached the end of me. Your father *hates* me, looks down upon me *and* my son. Every word that spews from his mouth is an insult. You have reprieve in your chores. But I…" She bit her lip again.

Reaching over her, he rubbed his hand along her back. Should he counter? It wasn't as if he didn't try to defend her. "Why, then, will you not let me speak for you?"

Hazel flashed again. "Not let you speak?"

"This evening. When he—"

"When our children were in the room? You wished that I allow you to unleash your temper upon the man? Say things you would regret? And might forever taint Samuel's opinion of you?"

He drew in a deep breath. And kept his tone low and calm. "That is not what I would have done, as you know."

"Nor would I—" Her voice softened and she relaxed into him.

"But I would not have you chastise me so publicly either." The words were out before he could stop them.

She jerked back, a movement so subtle it was nearly imperceptible.

Their gazes locked.

Were they not at an impasse? Who would give? Was he not in the right?

She could still get a rise out of him. In her desire to play peacemaker, she had overstepped and… wounded his pride. That pride of his!

Still, he had grounds to be upset, didn't he? It wasn't so long ago she scolded him for not speaking for her, and now, she impeded him from doing so. Impossible woman!

He wished he could pull away. Remove himself from their bed, from their room. But as soon as the thoughts entered his mind, he saw them for what they were—careless hopes born of his stubborn pride.

For as he looked into her face, he saw once more the woman he loved. The woman he vowed to cherish and love, for better or for worse. Had not God's word said that he should love her as he loved his own body? Would he be so quick to disengage from his foot because it offended?

No, these were the times that she, like his foot, needed more care, more attention.

He disentangled his arms until they were between them. And even as she pulled back, he grasped for her hands, forcing her to look at him. Drawing them to his chest once more, he forced his features to soften.

"You are right." His voice was but a whisper. That was the only way he could keep it gentle. "Forgive me my pride. And let me share your burden."

This time, when her eyes glistened as they met his, moisture welled and tears escaped.

"Would you?"

He bent his head toward hers. "Every day. For the rest of my life."

Amanda finished wiping the table after breakfast. The morning had been uneventful and a bit full at the same time. Brandon remained abed and Dan had gone for the doctor. Still, everything else in the house proceeded as if these things were not so.

As she returned the cloth to the kitchen, she met Cook's eyes over a basin of dishwater. "Need help?"

"No. You know I need this time to think."

Amanda nodded. Cook did her best thinking over a tub of soapy plates.

"Now get on out of here. Find something useful to do." Cook waved a wet hand toward the door. "Or not." She winked.

Not being useful.

That seemed rather nice.

Amanda stole away out the front door and to the back of the homestead. This place was rarely visited. She didn't mind that. In fact, it made this the perfect place to settle in for a little while. Some time to be 'useless.'

Just behind the house was an open space between a dirt road and a small grouping of trees. That space seemed a bit too exposed. Some of the windows in the homestead faced it. Anyone within could be watching her.

Slipping toward the tree line, she ducked between the branches and into what solitude they offered. Not far in, the vista opened again and she came upon a stream.

She found a large rock near the water's edge and, sitting upon its flat surface, removed the things that bound her feet and tested the blue coolness.

The unexpected chill made her jerk back, but

she did so long for the feel of the slow current. Dipping her toes in again, she forced her skin to adjust to the colder temperature.

As she sat, she gazed at the Arizona landscape. The mountains that were ever in the distance appeared in a splendid array of colors.

Could it be true that her simple, small faith could move them? As large and far away as they were? Dare she test it? Concentrating on one particular mound to the right, she stared at it and tried to move it.

Nothing.

Maybe she should close her eyes.

She did so. And, creasing her forehead, pressed her thoughts into moving the mountain.

Peeking through a narrow eye slit, she looked at her progress.

Nothing.

Was there doubt in her? Is that the reason she could not accomplish this? Did she truly think she *could* move this mountain? She did not know.

Easing the tension in her face, she leaned back, putting her arms behind her back to prop herself up.

Perhaps the mountains she should consider moving were not these in front of her, but the ones in her life. Brandon. His father. Their rift.

Could she move that mountain? Or would it, too, refuse to budge under her concerted efforts?

They were both so hard headed.

There was nothing *she* could do, that was certain.

But maybe…

If God did care about families…

And wanted Brandon and his father to find that common ground…

Then maybe.

Just maybe.

Father in Heaven,

I haven't been the best at bringing my requests to You. I have but a simple faith and am still learning. But I do trust You.

I know that if Brandon and his father are to reconcile, it will be because of You. For of their own devices, they are too far gone. There is stubbornness in one and pride in the other. But I beg You, Father, that You would do this thing.

And bring peace in my family.

Brandon sat in the great room, Louise at his feet, playing with her blocks.

The doctor had left and deemed him well enough. His foot, the man declared, had been well cared for and would heal. All the doctor wished was to leave him with a crutch to assist his maneuvering.

As Amanda helped Cook prepare the evening meal, he volunteered to keep watch over Louise.

He hadn't often the opportunity to spend time with his daughter. The duties of the ranch pulled at him much of the day and evening. A smile filled his face as he gazed at the tiny being, so pleased with her discoveries.

"How are you?" a voice broke into his thoughts.

It was Mother, stepping into the room on Father's arm.

Brandon's upturned lips faltered. But he kept a pleasant look about his features. There was no need to expect the worst. "I am well. The doctor believes I'll recover quickly."

"That *is* good news."

Father walked Mother to the nearby chair. After she was settled, Father took a seat opposite hers, farther away from Louise. Was it Brandon's imagination or did Father look upon the little girl with curiosity? Almost amusement? Perhaps that was a slight arch to his eyebrow.

Mother openly adored the child. "Look at those little hands. So small."

Brandon chuckled. "But they can do a lot of damage."

"Oh, you're telling me! Remember, I had two. Close in age. You and your sister worked together to keep me frazzled."

"It couldn't have been all that bad." Brandon met his mother's gaze.

"Of course not. You were both angels."

He shot her a sideways glance. *That* he did not believe either.

She laughed. "Except when you weren't."

Brandon laughed with her. It felt good to be at

ease with his parents. If only it could stay like this. Would it? Would Father let the pleasantness remain? Or would he open his mouth?

"She's…the child…she is putting that block in her mouth." Father leaned forward, his posture still as perfect as ever, and pointed at Louise's face.

Brandon glanced down. "Not to worry. She has teeth coming in. It helps her feel better."

Father caught Brandon's eyes. "But, she's chewing on that block."

Looking at Louise then at Father, Brandon nodded. "Yes, I see that."

Father adjusted his jacket as he leaned back. The way the man insisted on dressing for dinner was comical.

"Are you not concerned she will injure herself? Or the block?"

"The block is too big for her to hurt herself with, and until she gets teeth, she can't hurt the block."

Father continued to stare, but didn't say anything further.

Mother exchanged a look with Brandon.

Louise lost her hold on the block. It tumbled to the floor and out of her reach. She whined and searched for help.

Brandon reached down and picked her up.

Soothed, Louise seemed appeased by the rhythmic jostling of his knee.

Mother reached a finger toward her.

Louise took it and giggled.

"She reminds me of you, Brandon. Wouldn't you say?" Mother's gaze rested on Father.

"Oh, I shouldn't think she favors Brandon much at all. In fact, I wouldn't be surprised if…" Father's words died.

Brandon paused his leg's bouncing, meeting Father's eyes. "If what?"

Father waved a hand as he pulled out a pocket watch. "Never mind. Just the wonderings of an old man."

"And just what are these wonderings?"

"We don't need to—" Mother started, putting a hand on Brandon's arm.

"It is nothing." Father snapped the watch closed and tucked it away. "I spoke out of turn."

"You seem to be doing a lot of that lately." Brandon's words rushed out before he could stop them.

Father's eyes widened.

Mother's hand flew to her chest.

"Am I?" Father's brows went up. If possible, he sat straighter.

Brandon regretted his words, and he didn't. But he could do nothing now that they were out.

"If I am speaking out of turn, then it is because I am only concerned for your well-being."

"My well-being?" It was Brandon's turn to raise his brows.

"Yes. This…this woman." Father's hand flicked in the direction of the kitchen. "Who has somehow tricked you into marriage, perhaps by convincing you that this child is yours, is holding you back. You could be so much more. You were born to be so much more."

Mother gasped.

Brandon rose, eyes narrowing. He attempted to gather his thoughts before he spoke, but there was nothing, his mind was blank…a big red blank. "How dare you?"

"How dare I?" Father seemed as if he had never been more comfortable. As if they chatted about whether or not it would rain. "You are the one who ran from the family. Played cowboy for a while. And let some pretty face trap you."

"Ran? Play cowboy? Pretty face?" Brandon couldn't see straight. The room jerked from side to side.

He reached for the back of the chair. The world continued to spin. It would not be good if he dropped Louise. So, he set her on the floor.

"Let me be clear. I left to follow the only life that held any meaning for me. I did not want the life you planned. And I did not want your life. Why? Because I did not want to end up like you. A sad, sorry, unfeeling old man who had let the best years go right by." Brandon's volume rose with each word.

Father's face fell.

"And Amanda…let me tell you. She has more virtue than you will ever have. Or hope to have. And her children will remember her as kind. And good. And loving. Which is more than I can say for you."

"I see." Father struggled to stand.

Mother moved toward him.

He held out a hand to stop her.

Father's features were unreadable. But his eyes. There was something there. Something deep.

"Now that I know how you feel…I suppose there's nothing else to say." And without meeting Brandon's eyes, Father stepped from the room.

Mother turned to Brandon then. "What were you thinking?"

"What was *I* thinking?" Brandon arched a brow. What was she saying? Had she not heard the things he did? Where had she been?

"How could you say those things to your father?" Tears brimmed her eyes, and she turned away.

His heart ached for his mother and her impossible position, but still, he had to stand up for his family. "I don't mean you any ill will, Mother, but you must see… after what he said about Amanda, I—"

Mother's tear-streaked face jerked toward Brandon's, a flash in her eyes. "Don't you see? Your father is dying!"

CHAPTER FIVE

A Christmas Eve Thought

BRANDON SWALLOWED AGAINST a lump that had formed in his throat. "Dying?"

Mother wiped at her tears. "Yes." She fell into the chair.

He sat as well, putting his hands on her arm. "Tell me."

She shook her head. "There's nothing to tell. His body is weak. There is some sickness in him. Killing him. He grows weaker every day. The doctors don't know anything. They can't do anything."

"We must find other doctors."

Mother put her other hand on his. "Don't you think we've tried that? We've seen the best doctors back East. The foremost doctors in these fields. There is nothing to be done."

Tightness compressed Brandon's chest. It couldn't be true. Father? Dying? Wasn't he too stubborn to die?

"I know it's hard. But we have to accept it." Mother's gaze was elsewhere. Was she speaking to him? Or to herself?

He searched his feelings. His heart did hurt for his father. But why was Father so intent on spewing such venom? Was he attempting to manipulate Brandon? Trying to get him to return to Richmond? Take up the family practice after all this time? Leave his own family and everything he had built?

His mother's sobs filled his ears, and he put his own emotions and wonderings to the side. Wrapping an arm around his mother's shoulder, he offered what comfort he could.

Amanda stepped into the hall. Where had Samuel gone? He would be devastated if she rang the dinner bell without him. But where had he gotten off to?

A figure loomed ahead, leaning against a wall.

"Brandon?" Had he stumbled? Lost his crutch? Was he hurt?

She stepped toward him, reaching out a hand.

As she made contact with the figure, something told her it was not her husband.

The darkened silhouette jerked back and turned. Mr. Miller.

And he appeared to have been crying. Was that possible?

"Mr. Miller, are you well?"

"I am well enough." His voice was gruff. But he had an arm across his abdomen, and he was bent over slightly. She had never seen him with anything but the most perfect of posture.

Something in her heart twisted. In that moment, he seemed broken. And vulnerable.

"You must have something you should be doing." His eyes narrowed at her.

She shook her head. "Nothing as important as ensuring your comfort."

His brows rose. "My comfort?"

Nodding, she stepped toward him again. "Are you injured? You don't seem well."

"Indeed." He closed his eyes and leaned against the wall.

He didn't seem so intimidating right then. But rather like an overgrown child who had lost his way. Like Samuel, but taller. "Shall I call for Brandon?"

His eyes opened, and he held up a hand. "No!"

She observed him for a moment. Why did he react so strongly? Had something happened?

"I just…need to get to my room." He heaved a labored breath. "Perhaps you could help me."

Coming alongside him, she maneuvered an arm to slide around his waist.

His arm fell across her shoulders.

No sooner had his weight fallen on her than Brandon's voice boomed through the hallway. "Is it true?"

The larger man beside her turned. And she with him.

"What?"

Brandon now stood before them. How he had crossed such a distance with the crutch so quickly, she did not know. But here he was.

The weight of Mr. Miller's arm lifted, and he stood on his own two feet once more.

Proud.

Like father, like son.

"I want to know if it's true."

"What did your mother say?" Mr. Miller's voice had an edge to it.

"Enough." Brandon's features worked to harden, but there was a softness in his eyes. What had happened? "But I want you to tell me if it's true."

The muscles in Mr. Miller's jaw worked. Amanda watched them like small waves under his skin. For several moments, she thought he would not answer. He closed his eyes and drew in a ragged breath.

"Yes," he pushed out on an exhale. "It's true."

Brandon stared at his father. Was that a glimmer of moisture in his eyes? It was difficult to see in the dimness of the hallway.

"Why did you not tell us?" Brandon's voice was gentle. When was the last time he had spoken words in such a tone to his father?

"Because I didn't want you to know." Mr. Miller's eyes opened, and he met Brandon's gaze.

What were they saying? Amanda looked between the two men, silently regarding each other. What didn't Mr. Miller want them to know? The sadness in Brandon's eyes, the newfound slouch to Mr. Miller's shoulders.

It couldn't be.

Was it?

"What am I supposed to do with this?" Brandon broke the stillness.

Mr. Miller's features became placid for the briefest moment then hardened once again. "Nothing. Not one thing."

Brandon opened his mouth, but his father turned, nearly losing his balance.

Amanda gripped his arm closest to her.

As soon as he regained his footing, he held a hand up.

She backed away.

They could do nothing at that point but watch him move the rest of the way to his room, leaning heavily on the wall.

When Amanda shifted her focus to Brandon, his eyes were on the floor. Should she go to him? What could she say?

He sniffled.

"Brandon…" She took a step toward him.

His head jerked up. "It is no matter."

Her brows furrowed. "How can you say that?"

"It is what it is." His voice was soft, but firm. Did he truly believe that?

She sought his eyes, but he would not look at her.

He turned and moved off.

Should she follow? She did not know.

So, she backed up until the solid wall was behind her and sank to the floor.

And for just a moment, she allowed herself to fall apart.

Brandon sat on the porch. He held a block of wood in one hand, a whittling knife in the other. But he only absently moved the blade against the wood. His mind wasn't in it. Even as he gazed across the ranch, the place that held such beauty, such peace for him…it brought no joy. Not today.

How long had he sat out here? The sun hadn't been up when he found himself hobbling to this place of solitude. Had he intended to pray? Perhaps. But one needed clarity. Well, more clarity than he had.

So he sat. And stewed.

He became distantly aware of a wagon on the horizon. Its path cut through his property as it wound its way toward the homestead. But he wasn't worried. The cart, the horse, the occupants…all familiar to him. Perhaps more so than his own parents.

Uncle Owen and Cook.

So, Uncle Owen had recovered after all. It had been days since they had seen him.

A part of Brandon wondered if he was truly better or if he had a driving reason to come today.

No use wondering. He would know soon enough.

The wagon halted near the barn, and one of the ranch hands stepped out to take charge and help Uncle Owen and Cook out of their seats. And then the two were intent on the house, walking arm-in-arm toward him.

They mounted the stairs, but it slowed Uncle Owen's steps. That bad hip of his. Would it ever stop bothering him?

Perhaps Brandon should stand and offer to assist them, but he remained as he was, gazing over the pastureland and monitoring their progress. For he had his suspicions about what would be forthcoming. And he did not think it would be pleasant. He wanted the delusion for a little longer.

Soon, Uncle Owen stood next to him.

"How do you fare?"

Brandon wagged his head from side to side, still refusing to meet Uncle Owen's eyes. "All right, I suppose."

"That's not what I hear."

"Who you been talking to?" Brandon set his gaze on his whittling project. He had nearly stripped all the wood across the middle of the block. It was almost cut through.

"I have my sources."

Brandon nodded.

Silence fell between them. How long would he put off the inevitable?

"Won't you have a seat?" He indicated one of the chairs beside him.

"No. I won't. You're going to get off your rear and come into that house."

Manipulating the block in his hands, Brandon pretended to study it.

"Now." Uncle Owen's voice held more force.

Brandon looked at him.

There was no room for misunderstanding in the older man's expression either.

It was time.

Nodding, Brandon grasped his crutch and rose, though somewhat unsteady, to his feet.

"After you." Uncle Owen raised an arm toward the door.

They stepped into the house.

In the great room, Amanda and Mother had already assembled.

Cook offered him a half-smile and stepped from the room. What the devil…?

Brandon shot a look at Uncle Owen. "No."

The older man nodded. "It's high time. All the pieces. No one left out."

Amanda sat, hands folded in her lap, so unassuming. He didn't want her here. She didn't need to know. He didn't want her to know. How could he escape this? Perhaps Father wouldn't come. Yes, Father would refuse to have any part in this.

"Now, sit." Uncle Owen led Brandon to a chair. And then the older man hobbled down the hallway.

Raised voices echoed through the house. Brandon could catch a word here and there, but that was all.

When he looked up, Amanda's eyes were on him. She looked heavenly. Was this the only way?

In the moments that followed, though Brandon was doubtful how it happened, Father joined the contingency in the great room.

"There now." Uncle Owen heaved as he all but fell into a chair. "The whole lot of ya is here. Let's start speaking some truth."

Brandon met Father's gaze. Then he looked away.

Why did they have to rehash the past? What good would it do?

"There's some hurtin' and some hidin'. Time for some airing out."

Looking to the floor, Brandon was intent he would not be the one to start this. Because he was not the one who started it to begin with.

"Ain't any of ya' got anything to say?" Uncle Owen looked between Father and Brandon. "I mean, here you are…and you have the chance to say anything you ever wanted to say."

"Frankly, Owen, I think you should mind your

own business." Father stiffened, as he seemed to try to find some way to lean back and maintain his posture.

"Really? That's not what you said when you sent your son out here."

"Biggest mistake of my life," Father muttered. "If I had but known that summer of teenage fun would change a man's destiny, I would never had sent him."

"I only did what you asked. I taught the boy some responsibility." Uncle Owen waved a hand toward Brandon.

"That's laughable. First chance he had to prove it, he ran away."

Brandon rolled his eyes. "That is not true. I came home and did what you wanted. I finished law school. And all the while, I *told* you that I was not cut out for the law. You just wouldn't listen."

"Wouldn't listen? It was you who wouldn't listen! How can you forget your one and only case as my assistant? You had one assignment—follow through. Finish what you started. That's all I asked. And you packed up and left. In the middle of the trial. And me sitting in the courtroom waiting for you."

"That's *not* all you asked. You asked me to follow in your footsteps. To be just like you." Brandon's face heated.

"Not much chance of that." Father crossed his arms.

"You still don't understand."

Father's brows raised. "Enlighten me."

"I never wanted all of that. I still don't."

"Yes." Father seemed bored with the discussion. "You want to pursue a menial life of hard labor. A life where you will never know true success."

"That depends on how you define success." Feeling Amanda's eyes on him, he chanced a glance in her direction. She was smiling. He took courage from that.

"How would *you* define it?"

"Love. Loyalty. Friendship. Not having a broken relationship with your son." Though he had formed the words in anger, Brandon's tone was soft, his voice catching.

"You're the one who walked out." Father's words were still edged with anger. Or was it pain?

"To pursue my dreams."

"I gave you a choice."

"And I chose. I'd choose the same again if I could."

Father's glare was hard on Brandon. But there was sadness there, too.

"Not because I don't love you, Father. But because I have to be true to myself."

The older man's graying expression settled on Brandon's. For a moment, Brandon knew he would give. That with better understanding, they would overcome their challenges.

Yet Father turned away. "Owen, you push too hard."

Rising, Father swayed.

Mother was on her feet in a moment. "Charles!"

He gently pushed her back. "I can manage."

And he stepped from the room as easily as he had entered.

Was he affected by any of it?

The tree appeared every bit as wonderful as Brandon hoped. Except that it had not been by his hand. Cutie and Slim had gone out and selected another tree, cut it, and brought it to the homestead. He'd had no part in the process.

Still, it was lovely. The greenery fit well with the decorations Amanda had selected for the great room, and the meager presents were tucked snuggly underneath. What precious little trimming they had done highlighted its significance.

He could measure Louise's height by the branches that were already suffering from her reach. Surely the lower portion of the tree would be brown before they had tired of it.

The smell of burning wax filled his senses as Amanda lit candles around the great room. Was it time?

He glanced into the dining room.

All the plates were cleared, and Samuel shuffled in with the oversized family Bible in his arms. He was used to seeing Cutie, Dan, Slim, Uncle Owen, and Cook around the table, but they would share this Christmas Eve around Cook and Uncle Owen's tree.

Mother and Father stepped in from the hallway.

He had not seen Father since yesterday when they had argued. The stubborn man had kept to his room. How Mother ever convinced him to come out, Brandon would never know.

They sat across the room from Brandon, and Father avoided his gaze. On purpose? Or was he truly as interested in the candlelight as he seemed?

He didn't look good. His skin seemed ashen. How had it become so much grayer in just a day?

A wriggling bundle was plopped into Brandon's lap.

Louise.

Amanda winked and moved toward Samuel, already settled in front of the tree. Sitting on the floor beside him, she looked over his shoulder as he opened the massive book.

Brandon was thankful for the distraction from his parents.

Louise gurgled and reached for his nose with a wide grin.

"Is everyone ready?" Samuel said. His voice timid and soft.

Brandon looked around Louise and watched as Amanda nudged Samuel with her arm and whispered in his ear.

"It's time for the Christmas Story." This time, he was much louder, more confident.

Mother and Father's conversation halted, and Brandon set Louise to sit in his lap, facing her brother.

Samuel beamed at his success.

Amanda nudged him again and indicated the large Bible.

And he began to read. The story was one Brandon had heard so many times. Of Mary and Joseph. Of the angel appearances and instructions. How they went to Bethlehem and there was no room in the inn for—

"What?" Samuel stopped himself.

Brandon was pulled out of the story.

"No room for Jesus?"

"They didn't know the baby in Mary's tummy was Jesus," Amanda explained.

"But they did see she was going to have a baby?" He looked at her, eyes wide and brows nearly joined.

"I'm sure they did." Amanda leaned back.

"And they didn't make room for her?"

Brandon wanted to laugh at his childlike questions, but he was too intrigued by their conversation.

"It's strange to think about that. But if they didn't have any room, they couldn't make the room."

"But Pa made room. He built a room!" His eyes shone as he looked across.

Brandon couldn't help the swell of pride in his chest.

"Yes. But that takes time. Mary and Joseph needed room that night."

"Couldn't they sleep on the floor? Or camp out?"

All good questions. How would Amanda answer them?

"I think that people were already sleeping on the floor. And it wasn't safe to camp out. But God provided, right?"

Samuel's eyebrows scrambled again as he thought.

"In the stable, remember?"

Louise chose that moment to bite Brandon's finger, but he stifled his yelp. He didn't wish to intrude on this endearing exchange.

"When it comes to His plans, God will always make a way."

God will always make a way.

Truly?

How could he even think that? Of course he knew it to be true. Those words penetrated his heart, long since shrouded in a web of hurt and anger. Would God make a way for him and his father? He didn't see how. But wasn't that what faith was all about?

CHAPTER SIX

Christmas Draws 'Nigh

THE HOUSE WAS silent at last. Samuel and Louise had calmed and surrendered to sleep after the excitement of the evening. Brandon would have bet against it, but Amanda had some manner of magic she worked upon them.

He stepped from their bedroom into the darkened house. Where had she slipped off to? There was one gift he wanted to give outside of the mayhem that was the present-opening storm. His hard wrought, hand hewn offering for his wife. How he had found the time to put into it, he still wasn't sure. But he had made the time.

Balancing the twine-bound box on his good side

and maneuvering with the crutch on the other, he made his way toward the porch—Amanda's favorite place to take in the quiet evening moments. Was she expecting him?

It took some effort to work the door latch with his hands both occupied as they were, but he managed. He stepped onto the porch soon thereafter.

The evening air was chillier than he had expected, but it was pleasant enough. A clear sky greeted him. Was it the same sky that had shown upon Mary and Joseph that long-ago night?

Turning toward the bench he and Amanda so often shared, he found it vacant. But the seat beside it was not. And the features which studied him were none other than his father's.

A wave of uncertainty flushed through him, followed by a rush of heated anger. Should he just turn back inside? Avoid the confrontation altogether? Seek out Amanda for the rendezvous he had hoped for? This was certainly not what he wanted.

His father's eyes remained leveled upon him, as if waiting for his decision. Did Father wish him to stay? What was he up to? Would he speak if Brandon lingered?

In his musings, Brandon stood for several moments. His gaze still on Father. Gauging the man the same as he did Brandon.

The older man's brow arched, and Father shifted his focus toward the horizon. Then his eyes closed and he leaned his head back. Was he tired? Weak?

Something cracked in the wall around Brandon's heart. It was impossible to discern if it came from the outside or the inside.

When it comes to His plans, God will always make a way.

Brandon set the gift on a nearby rocking chair and hobbled to his and Amanda's bench.

Father did not so much as flinch.

Though Brandon did not want to, his gaze swept over the man. How had Brandon not noticed how much thinner he was? His clothes fairly hung on him now. Shoulders protruding eluded to the bony nature of his form.

Even his face... Was there any excuse for Brandon to have not seen it in his features? Hollow cheeks and darkened eyes told the story of a man losing a physical battle. This was not the man Brandon knew.

"Are you going to say something or just gawk at me?" The voice was not harsh. Rather his words came out soft, resigned. Was he now resigned to his fate?

"Is there no fight left in you?"

Eyes that were now best described as gray opened. They were hard upon Brandon. "No fight left? You have *no* idea how I've..." His lips trembled ever so slightly, and he pressed them together. His lids closed, and he rested his head back once more. "You wouldn't understand."

Brandon swallowed, biting back words that forced their way to the surface. Angry words. Why did this man bring out the worst in him?

He pulled in a breath and let it out. *Lord, give me the words. Calm my thoughts, banish my hurt, my ire, and let me see Your way.*

Opening his eyes, Brandon studied the wood grain of the crutch, moving his fingers along the smooth surface.

"You're right. I don't." Brandon sighed.

Father grunted, raising his head, looking across the field once more.

"But I would…" Brandon turned toward him. "If you would tell me."

Father blinked. Were his eyes glistening? It was there and then it was gone. Controlled. The older man set his gaze upon his son. His gray orbs probing. Was he testing the veracity of Brandon's statement?

Brandon did not waver. "Much has been said between us. Much to be regretted. On *both* our parts. And there is much room for understanding."

Father's gaze hardened for but a moment, then it softened.

And he nodded.

"We have to start somewhere. Why not here? Why not now?" An ache opened in Brandon's chest.

Why had he made himself so vulnerable? Sure his father had agreed with him, but that didn't mean the man was ready to put the past behind them. Even if he could.

Brandon opened his mouth to revise his statement. To say something…anything that would protect himself should his father take a stab at his exposed heart.

But he closed it. On this precipice, it was a point of trust. Not with his earthly father, but his heavenly one.

And God had never failed him.

His father eyed him; a mix of emotion playing across his features. Then they became placid.

Brandon swallowed.

Father set a hand on Brandon's.

"Then let it begin…with me."

Amanda's eyes opened. Her husband's face was the first thing that greeted her. It had not been the last thing she saw before falling asleep.

After putting Samuel to bed, she had discovered Brandon on the porch with his father. Prudence begged she step out and determine if the interchange required a mediator. But something had stopped her. Perhaps it was time they speak just the two of them. Come what may.

What had happened in the end?

The urge to set her hand upon Brandon's face and wake him was nearly irresistible.

But she could not.

He may be tired from a late night of words with the man.

And even more so if they had been emotionally charged.

Rolling onto her back, she looked at the ceiling. Christmas Day had come. A day of peace on earth and goodwill for all mankind. But she felt anything but celebratory.

Drawing in a breath, she let it out slowly and sent up a prayer for unity in her family.

"Merry Christmas."

Turning her head, she met the dark brown eyes of her beloved. "Merry Christmas." She offered him a smile. "Is it truly?"

He reached to the bedside table opposite her. When he faced her once more, he had a brown package held together with a clumsy bow. But the grin on his face told of his pride in whatever lay within. "For you."

She pushed back in the bed until she was sitting against the headboard. "A present, but the present opening—?"

"I wanted you to open it when it was just you and me." He struggled into a seated position as well.

Setting the odd-looking package in her lap, she touched the rough brown paper with tentative fingers.

"Don't do that." He rolled his eyes. "Tear it."

She reached for the bow and pulled at one of the hanging strings. It gave way. A little. A tug at the other yielded the same result.

He shrugged. "I guess I'm not the best at bows. Just rip it!"

Grabbing for the twine, she yanked at it. It still wouldn't give. Pulling and pulling, she couldn't get any more room. Not even enough to slide it off the side and get it out of the way.

He groaned and reached into her lap, easily snapping the string in two.

"Thank you," she said, her words slow. And she attacked the rough paper next. Only moments later, she dug into the center and revealed her prize.

A plaque. It was carved with curved edges and the words 'THE MILLERS' displayed in bold on the surface. The wood had been sanded and stained to a beautiful dark cherry.

She picked it up.

And something clattered.

Curious.

At the bottom of the plaque was an iron loop. And attached to the loop were hearts shaped from horseshoe nails.

"What?" Her brows furrowed.

"Count them." He leaned in, his breath warmed the side of her face.

"Four." She pulled them up with a hand, examining them.

"One for each of us: me, you, Samuel, and Louise. The Miller Family. And there's room for more." His lips swept across her cheek.

"They are beautiful!" She shifted to look into his eyes. "*It* is beautiful!"

His mouth caught hers, and they did not speak for some moments.

"Merry Christmas," he said once more as he pulled back.

She nodded, her eyes still closed.

His hand ran through her hair.

Her eyes opened. "Is it?" She repeated her question.

"Is it what?" His voice was husky.

"A merry Christmas?"

His brows furrowed. "I don't understand."

She set the plaque down. "I saw you and your father on the porch last night."

He nodded.

"Is there hope?"

Bringing his hands up, he cupped her face between them. "Even better — there is peace."

"Truly?" She blinked back the tears that sprang immediately.

"Upon my life. All is as it should be."

She searched his eyes for but a moment before throwing arms around his shoulders. "I prayed it would be so. But I feared my faith was too small."

He pulled back. "What did I tell you? That's the kind of faith that can move mountains."

"So you did." She smiled. "So you did."

Also from Sara R. Turnquist

CHAPTER ONE

Lost

MARIENA GU ACHI gazed at the sun descending to the point where the sky met land. The purples, pinks, and orange filled her vision. It stole her breath. And firmed its claim on her heart.

Still, a sickness settled in her midsection. How would they ever make it?

Her brother stirred beside her. So young. So trusting.

He relied on her. Needed her to find a way. But that didn't mean she could.

Her heart weighed heavy, its movements becoming laborious.

The chance of her and her brother being captured by Apache and sold into slavery…or worse… lay as a yoke across her shoulders.

That was if a coyote didn't find them first.

How would she manage? It was simply too far.

And everything stood against her. She bit her lip. Perhaps the pain would stave off the tears threatening to fall.

Nisto didn't need that.

No, he couldn't know that she was lost.

That *they* were lost. And hopeless.

Even if he tried, Cutie could no longer hear the sound of cattle. Noises that were the staple of his typical day would not fill this one. And he so needed a break from the drudgery of normalcy.

Oh, it wasn't that he didn't love his life on the ranch. He had become…accustomed to it. Comfortable with it. Where else would he want to be?

But today was his.

More often than not, he allowed himself to be drawn into Wharton City in his off time. But lately, he found solace in the dusty trails that lay far from the reaches of the city. Or the ranch.

Unexplored.

Untried.

Not a soul for miles.

He pushed his painted horse harder, faster. Striving for that peace he never seemed able to quite reach.

Hadn't Brandon started to trust him again? While his boss spoke of forgiveness and what that meant, it seemed impossible. Cutie had wronged the man. And the rancher had nearly lost everything: his ranch, his wife…and his very life. All because Cutie got a little restless. A little greedy.

And for what? A handful of crisp bills to gamble away?

His chest ached. He shoved the thoughts to the edge of his consciousness, but they would move no further.

A stream appeared off to the right. The horse needed little prompting to veer that direction. How long had he pressed her?

The animal slowed as they neared the clear flowing water. Still, the thundering of the hoof beats drowned out all other sound.

Even when the mare had all but stopped, just short of the cool water, the pounding remained. Did Cutie's own heart race so wildly?

Sliding from the saddle, he laid a hand to the horse's slick muscled neck. A layer of sweat betrayed just how hard she had worked for him.

Why had he pushed her so? He knew better. It would not be safe to run her like this on the way back. She would not likely survive it.

Clicking his tongue, he pulled gently on the reins and led her the short distance remaining to the stream.

While she drank, he crouched and soaked his bandana. Wiping it across his face, he relished the coolness against his overheated skin. Had he been running from the devil? Or something worse?

He frowned and gazed at the swirling water.

Something…there on the edge of his consciousness, threatened to creep forth. Was this what he worked so hard to elude?

Dare he, in this place, test this thing?

Settling back on his backside, he rested his elbows on his knees and squinted at the great rock formations in the distance—seeming to have been painted unique shades of purples and reds by God's own hand.

God.

Now there was a thought.

God.

Indeed.

He rubbed his face against his shoulder and caught sight of movement further downstream by the water's edge.

What was that?

Perhaps nothing. He focused again on the butte. Still, it nagged on the edge of his awareness. Something *was* there. Or someone. Had he been followed?

He almost laughed. Who would care to? He wasn't important enough.

Glancing to that side, though he kept his head turned forward, he sensed more than saw motion.

He jerked his head toward it.

There. In the brush. Not even a good hiding place.

He rose, keeping an eye on the bush as he did so, and moved his hand to hover over his gun. "Who's there?"

No answer.

He shot a quick glance at his horse. She grazed nearby. Should he walk her over with him?

Backing up, he grabbed for the dangling leather and secured it to a tree branch. Never once taking his eyes off the place where he had noted the movement.

"Nothing? No answer?" He took careful steps forward, a hand on his revolver.

As he came closer, he picked up on more sounds. Small movements. Whispers.

"Show yourself!"

The movements stilled.

His steps arced wide to come alongside the bush. He pulled his gun from its resting place as he came around to the back side of the obstructing bush.

When all was exposed to him, he found two sets of deep brown eyes staring wide at him.

Mariena stared at the revolver pointed at her face. She tightened her lips into a thin line and hardened her jaw.

No fear.

With steady movements, she shifted Nisto until he was behind her. Though it mattered little. If this man wanted to kill them, he would simply shoot her and then Nisto.

Still, she could not help but create a barrier between the weapon, its owner, and her young brother.

The man eyed them. What was he thinking? Why didn't he just do what he intended?

He cocked the gun then lowered it. "What the devil?"

The devil? Did he think she was a devil? Perhaps it was true that the white man thought all her people nothing but savages. And her…a she-devil.

Mariena forced her features to remain neutral. Best not give the man anything else to support his assumptions.

"You are going to get killed all sneaking around behind bushes."

She continued to watch him.

Nisto whimpered, still curled in a ball behind her.

The man ran a hand over his face. "Great. No English."

Dare she? What good would it do for her to expose her language skills? Why shouldn't she?

The best weapons are those kept secret. One of Father's wisdoms.

But this man might have food. Or may even help them. They had evaded death for too long already. They could not elude it much longer.

Not reasonably.

This man had not ended their lives when he'd had the chance. Perhaps he could help. Perhaps he would.

"Ah…just never mind. I'll forget I ever saw ya'." The man waved his hand in their direction and turned toward his horse.

"Mister Sir," she said. The words sounded strange, even to her. Heavily accented by her native tongue. Could he even understand her?

He jerked around, eyes on hers once again. "What?"

She rose with hesitancy.

Nisto put his legs under him and started to lift his body as well.

Shifting, she admonished him in their language and held a hand down. "No! Let me talk to him first."

Nisto stilled and then crouched once more.

"You speak English?"

"Yes." Best to keep her words few. Better he didn't find out how simple and limited her English was. Would it anger him?

"Who are you? Where are you from? What are you doing out here?"

Her head spun with the many words. She worked to decipher his questions. "We are of Tohono O'odnam."

"The Desert Indians."

She nodded.

"I thought what of ya' didn't go to Mexico headed to San Xavier to the Reservation."

A great ache filled her chest. She looked to the ground. It wasn't for him to see.

"So?"

She looked off to the side. "My nation is split, as you say. And my tribe started the trip to Mexico."

"You took a wrong turn." He made a snort-like laugh.

Her eyes jerked up toward his. There was indeed humor on his face. Would she ever smile again? "We were attacked."

His smile fell.

"My brother and I are all that is left of my village."

"I'm sorry."

She folded herself in her arms, shivering despite the warmth of the sun bearing down on them.

"Are you headed for the reservation now?"

Looking down at her arms, she worked to control her features. "We are lost."

"In this wilderness?" His tone betrayed his shock. "Do you realize how dangerous that can…?"

His words trailed off. Why had he not finished his question?

She turned her gaze up toward him once again.

Their eyes met for the briefest moment before he looked away.

And she understood. The man felt sorry for them. Pitied them. Her heart sank. This was far worse than the fear of the gun. The heaviness in the pit of her stomach weighed that of a thousand stones.

Must she appear so helpless?

She closed her eyes. What choice did she have? Without a home, without her parents, her family, her tribe…she *was* helpless.

To read more of Cutie and Mariena's story,
pick up a copy of

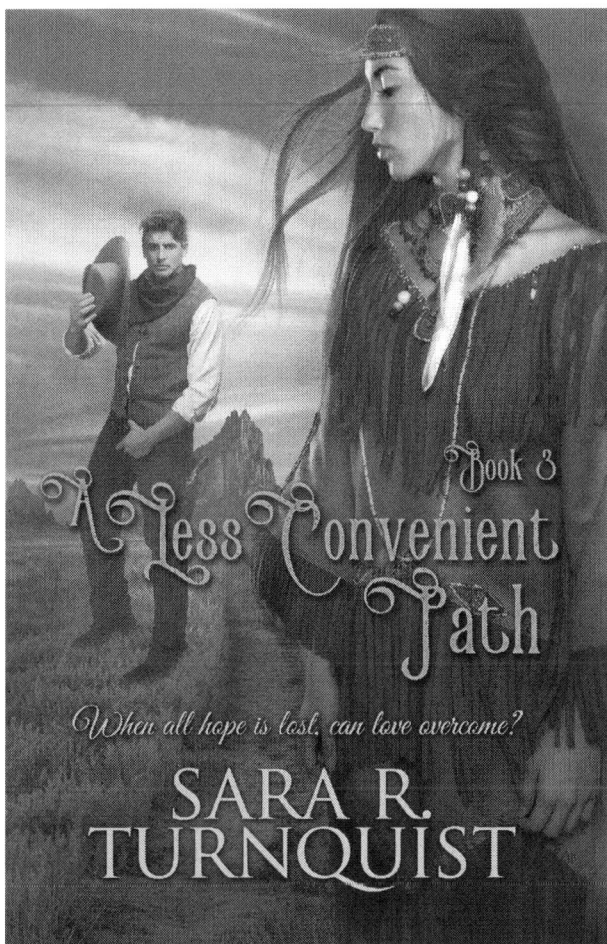

Book 3

A Less Convenient Path

When all hope is lost, can love overcome?

SARA R.
TURNQUIST

ACKNOWLEDGMENTS

Wow…when I started working on this Christmas novella, I hoped it would happen, but had my doubts. And here it is. There are so many people who made this possible and I cannot name everyone who encourages my career and prays over me. This list would be longer than the book! I am truly blessed. But there are some that I will thank by name.

Julie Sherwood, my editor, thanks for keeping me honest. I know you put everything you can into your work and it makes my work shine.

Cora Graphics, your work never ceases to amaze me! I am so demanding and you deliver. Every time.

The photographer who makes me look good, VerBull Photography, I know I'm taking full advantage of your skills.

The Clarksville Christian Writers, my critique group, thanks for your thoughts on my writing and the encouragement you dish out every week. Keeps me coming back for more.

Hannah Conway, I always take the time to thank you because you always deserve it. Your unending support makes me believe this thing is possible.

My husband and number one fan, thank you for

continuing to see potential in me. And for helping make my dream a reality.

For my sister, you make me want to be better. For my dad, you make me feel so good to have achieved this dream of writing. For my mom, I will love you forever. And for my kids, you give me every reason to smile.

Last, but certainly not least, my readers, you give me a reason to keep writing.

Check out what else is available from Sara R. Turnquist

A Convenient Risk
An Inconvenient Christmas
A Less Convenient Path

The Lady Bornekova
The Lady and the Hussites

Hope in Cripple Creek
Christmas in Cripple Creek

The General's Wife

Off to War

Leaving Waverly, a novella

Trail of Fears

Sara is a coffee lovin', word slinging, Historical Romance author whose super power is converting caffeine into novels. She loves those odd little tidbits of history that are stranger than fiction. That's what inspires her. Well, that and a good love story.

But of all the love stories she knows, hers is her favorite. She lives happily with her own Prince Charming and their gaggle of minions. Three to be exact. They sure know how to distract a writer! But, alas, the stories must be written, even if it must happen in the wee hours of the morning.

Sara is an avid reader and enjoys reading and writing clean Historical Romance when she's not traveling.

Please follow along with her journey through her newsletter at: http://saraturnquist.com/list

Happy Reading!